A GOLDEN TRIANGLE

A FRIENDS4LIFE MYSTERY

OLIVIA VIYELLA

World Castle Publishing, LLC
Pensacola, Florida
Copyright © 2024 Olivia Viyella
Paperback ISBN: 9798891262140
eBook ISBN: 9798891262157
First Edition World Castle Publishing, LLC, June 10, 2024
http://www.worldcastlepublishing.com

Cover: Cover Designs by Karen
Cover-designs-by-karen.com
Editor: Karen Fuller

To Maite, my very real Mo.

CHAPTER ONE

OLLIE

"Donut, donut. When does that darn donut go in effect again? Can you take a tiny look-see at this receipt, darling?"

"How many times do I have to tell you? All the information's online. It's all there." Might as well save my breath. My sister is many things: A devoted mom, a fantastic cook, a canny seamstress, an elegant hostess. The whole domestic diva package. But computer savvy ain't one of them. "By the way, I just spoke to Trey."

Mo ignores me and continues to study the paper in her hand with a deep frown that brings her carefully depilated eyebrows together. It's a sign of her distress that she forgets her policy of "No frownies!" which she always calls out whenever I fall into a brown study. There's been times when we've come to blows, actual blows when she insists on trying to smooth my forehead with one of her impeccably manicured nails. "Bubble Bath," is her favorite these days, I think.

She doesn't even respond to the deep, dramatic sigh that underscores my words. My attempt to distract her with a mention of her son doesn't work, either. Who can blame her? These days, our pharmacy charges, like our worries, seem to expand like a pair of elastic-waisted jeans after one of Mo's legendary Thanksgiving meals.

And speaking of good eats, we both catch the scent coming from the kitchen at the same time. "Ollie, I left you in charge!" My sister then disappears in a cloud of Joy, the perfume that has been her trademark since she was a teenager. That would be years and years and years ago, many more decades than I care to remember.

I'm not being catty here. Maureen Marie Martin… why stop there? Let's pile them all up; the woman's a pack rat… Maureen Marie Martin O'Bryan Esposito Novak—that walking billboard for most ethnic groups of Chicago, best pronounced "ednics," of course—is my baby sister. As the only girls in a family of six children, Mo and I have always been close. But ever since she suggested we share her home in Florida, we've become closer. Two peas in the proverbial pod.

Which is why I'm dreading the conversation that is coming. We must find more ways to economize. We got rid of the premium channels. Woe is me. When the TV died an inglorious death, there was no replacing it. All our books come from the library. And don't get me started on the topic of our electronics. Mine, I should say. Unplugged Mo would happily keep the United States Postal System in business for the next millennium.

So, if cable series, a new TV, the latest bestsellers, replacing my phone and my laptop— "vintage" the infants at the store dared call it, last time I took it in for service at the Apple store—if it's all out of the question, I repeat, how do I break the news to her that expensive grocery items are next on the chopping block? Pun fully intended.

She, a widow, far from her children and grandkids, whose kitchen is her sole remaining pleasure in the sunset of her life. That, by the way, is Mo's way of explaining, to all and sundry, her interest in fancy French cookery. Lavish dishes that I, for one, am more than happy to consume; let's be fair.

There's no way, however, we can put off talking about our budget. The situation is now an emergency. Either we find a way to retrench even more, or come December, we may have to move out. And rent the cottage for the season. Make that the Season. To hear some of the people on our side of town say it, the period between January and April comes with sparkles and bows and unicorns.

Don't get me wrong. It is a considerable asset, the yellow and white cottage on 14th Avenue South between Gulf Shore Boulevard and Gordon Drive in Ye Olde Naples. "Don't forget to pronounce the e in Olde," as I often tell some of our snobbier neighbors. Our location puts us a couple of steps from the beach and the Naples high life, which is plenty high around here, most particularly in winter.

But the cottage is Mo's only asset. All she has left after her disastrous marriage to a swindler and a cheat. The Chase Incident. Our term—okay, mine—for the romantic miscalculation that emptied my once-very-comfortable sister's bank account. As for me, Leslie's pension and his Social Security seem to evaporate these days, even as they're being direct deposited.

It's on days like today when I realize I am not one to talk. If Mo's third husband was her financial undoing, my downfall was grief. When Leslie "Jack" Howard—only I was allowed to call him by his given name, our private joke—died, I sold everything. Yes, know-it-all that I am, I didn't listen to any words of advice.

Gone in a flash was the house in Beverly. And the Oak Lawn two-flats that my husband, as is often the case with Chicago firemen, had carefully invested in for our retirement. Sold at bargain basement prices. And then I socked all that money away in accounts that cannot be touched for another few years.

As things now stand, Mo's cottage and my investments

will have to be our nest egg for our old-old age. Not to be confused with our teenage-senior years, as my sister insists on calling our present stage in life. But between our shrinking bank statements, increasing expenses, property taxes, our many medications, and maladies—oh, lord, those—opening a bill these days is becoming a chore to be dreaded.

As it is for so many of our female friends. "The ladies of a certain age and uncertain birthdays." That's another Moism. Many of them, I am well aware, are a lot less fortunate than the two of us.

So, having to leave our home for part of the year may soon become a reality. But here's the catch: Cash-strapped as we are, how would we come up with the deposit to rent a cheaper place on the other side of Tamiami just as the hordes of snowbirds descend upon us?

We'd have to ask Trey or his sister, Dr. Molly, for help. But Mo won't entertain *that* idea. I get the same reaction as when I suggest she sell the cottage. Prime real estate. "Oh, you, Ollie! Out of the question!" Mo has made that abundantly clear she is not parting with the house that's been in the family for four generations of a tribe unusually gifted with long memories. Apparently, the O'Bryans are champions at the fine Irish art of keeping score, be it grudges or happy remembrances of days by the shore.

Financial ruin or not, my usually easy-going sister is determined to do things her way. That means, absolutely no pleas for financial help from anybody. She will keep what is left of her kids' heritage i-n-t-a-c-t, as Salinger once wrote in another context. Yeah, meet a librarian, get tons of book quotes.

Oh, well. I hear dinner's ready. And Bert is barking and running around in happy circles at the continuing aromas coming from the kitchen.

***

"This time, Mo, you outdid yourself," I mumble, still licking my lips, as I push away from the table.

"Thanks, dear heart. But all the credit goes to the butcher. He totally gets how a free-range pork belly should be scored. But I will say the fresh figs were a nice touch..."

"Now that you mention it," I say, dabbing the last remnants of chocolate mousse from my mouth. "There's something we need to discuss —"

"Will you look at that?" No dummy her, my sister jumps from her chair and flourishes one hand towards the patio. She continues then with even more enthusiasm than usual. "Come on, Ollie. You're always saying we need more exercise. Let's go for a walk to the pier. Right now!"

I follow her pointing hand. Up above, the sky is gold and pink, the fleecy clouds as delicately tinted as one of the porcelain shepherdesses that lived on Mom's vanity table for ages. Mo catches my quick glimpse towards the pile of books by my chair.

"Murder and mayhem can wait a little longer. Let's go breathe some fresh sea air," she insists. "No, not you," Mo adds in Bert's direction, almost in the same breath. "So sorry, baby cakes. You know the rules."

Is there a dog alive who doesn't understand the word "walk"? And not to brag unduly, but our rescue is way smarter than your average dog. Your average human, in fact. Still, it is a strict policy at the Naples Pier that no dogs are allowed. And the Martin sisters abide by the rules, for the most part.

While I deal with the dejected Bert, who, like me, is not averse to treats, Mo goes off to get ready. When she said, "right now," of course, she meant after a quick look in the mirror. Dishes can wait. Lipstick and earrings? Never!

***

As we head north, I forget my worries for a moment. It is a beautiful, breezy evening. Or as breezy an evening as you're going to get in late June in Florida. Still, the wind has picked up since I got home from work. The candy-like aroma of coconut-scented sunblock rises from the mass of people around us.

It is only a couple of blocks to our destination, but the streets are packed with visitors. Summer is always a festive time in Naples. The snowbirds may be gone, but it is the time for families with vacationing children to come visit. The babble of happy voices increases as we approach the 12th Avenue entrance. At first glance, it seems as if the whole of the tourists of Southwest Florida have descended on the pier today.

Not that it can't handle the invasion. Weathered brown and straight, the structure stretches into the Gulf for a thousand feet. Powdered sugar sands extend, as far as the eye can see, on both sides, the expanse dotted with bathers. A green line separates their towels and umbrellas from a strip of backyards.

On this stretch of Naples, some of the city's most impressive estates border the public beach. Go figure, pay a gazillion dollars for your house and have it open to the eyes of all and sundry. It would drive me mad, being stared at all the time by the hoi polloi. And I say that with the greatest respect as a card-carrying member of the great unwashed.

The walkway is as mobbed this evening as it usually is on any sunny evening. The vibe is so mellow, so Florida, I don't even direct my usual "tsk, tsk, tsk," accompanied by a shake of my head at the few visitors who have dogs by their sides. This is no time to be looking around, not yet. Not until it's safe.

Much as my sister and I love a long stroll on the venerable wharf, once we trod the wooden planks, it is our unspoken policy to keep our eyes front and center.

As it turns out, the Naples Pier, where fishing licenses

are not required, attracts tons of fishermen in all kinds of weather. I understand mackerel, pompano, and sea trout are plentiful in the nearby waters. And so are the clouds of pelicans that circle the skies around the balustrade in the hopes of stealing a random fish from a fisherman's hand.

Which is why it is also routine the sight of some pitiful bird—cries of distress rending the air—flapping its wings hysterically, a cruel hook embedded on his neck or even its pouch. I have to say the fishing community always rushes to help them. But the possibility of seeing it happen is too awful to chance during what is meant to be a leisurely evening stroll. Thus, we tend to keep our eyes front and center until we reach a secure spot, one away from fishing lines.

That is, I do. At least today. Very soon, I spy, from the corner of my little eye, another familiar sight. Not two feet away, a man is flirting with Mo. His skin, tanned to a deep walnut, glistens against a white shirt, open at the throat. Flashing white teeth, check; dark hair—oiled, I swear—check; expensive-looking gold aviator sunglasses, check. He appears, in fact, to have complied with all the requirements of the aspirant to a gigolo. And for heaven sakes, who wears gold chains these days?

And just as predictably, my sister is returning her most alluring glances, complete with batted eyelashes. Experience has taught me the uselessness of saying anything. Mo will only stare back at me with a patented "Who me? He started it!" But before I can even try tugging at her tunic sleeve, a cry of "Dolphins!" rises in the balmy evening air.

The call is followed, almost immediately, by a rush of people running towards the end of the pier, the best spot to see the frolicking fish. I know, I know, they're mammals, not fish. I was also told once by a young marine biologist that dolphins' behavior towards seals, even humans, demonstrates the dangers of anthropomorphism. Dolphins are not as nice as we all think they are. Good taste prevents me from saying any more on that topic.

Still, a pod of surfacing dolphins is an irresistible sight. As they breach the turquoise waters with those wide, goofy smiles, it is difficult to reject the thought that springs to mind: Those fish are truly having the time of their lives. So, there you have it, sue me.

***

Maybe the push came from somebody in the crowd, still rushing to catch a glimpse of the dolphins. Perhaps it was a tot running excitedly back to grandma, ice cream cone in hand, like the tiny maniacs they all are. The children, I mean. Although I've met quite a few gaga grannies in my day. Or maybe it was one of the random dogs on the pier today.

In hindsight, however, all I can say is that the cuff of Mo's fuchsia-and-white tunic is almost within the grasp of my fingers, one moment. The next second, it is nowhere to be found. Instead, there is my sister, face down on the Brazilian walnut wooden floor of the Naples Pier, immobile at my feet.

"911! Somebody dial 911!" The words rise in the air before I can make any sense of the sight. Are they mine? I can't tell. I then sense more than see, a wide space open around us, even as a chattering mob gathers around the perimeter.

"What happened?"

"Some old lady dropped dead."

"Did somebody call 911?"

"Darling, please. Please, Mo, talk to me."

"Load it on YouTube, quick!"

BETTY

Few things I enjoy more in this new life of mine than stepping outside and seeing the Gulf opening before me like an aquamarine evening gown embroidered with silver and white spangles. A small sailboat, sails fully unfurled, in the distance, is a sight capable of making my heart sing.

Most days, I begin with a cup of coffee on the back. Sunny or cloudy, doesn't matter. I eat my lunch back there, too. Manny and I even close the evening with a couple of drinks as we stare at the sea and a toast of long standing. "Here's to us!" it goes. To which one of us always responds: "And perdition to our enemies!"

Not that we have any. Enemies, I mean. Business rivals, once upon a time. Lots of competitors, some underhanded, on occasion, that, too. But we don't even have those these days. Like very few people I know, my husband and I have been blessed beyond reason. Our children are well and busy at their chosen professions. We have lovely grandchildren. Our health is excellent, and our finances... Let's just say my present life is the stuff movies are made of.

Which makes it so much harder for me to confess any dissatisfaction to my friends and family. Or at least without coming across as an entitled whiner. Sigh.

***

Today, with my husband away, after a dinner of bread, cheese, and fruit, I take myself for a stroll. Manny suggested Port Royal, but I put my foot down. I need to step outside and see life around me. "Trees and birds and grass, beautiful. But first, people," as Ma used to say.

I step onto the beach, right outside my backyard, below a sky that is drenched in color. A riot of blues and pinks and golds band the horizon, like something out of one of those musicals Ma and I loved. "Seven Brides for Seven Brothers." "The Unsinkable Molly Brown." I suppose that's why I'm remembering her more than ever. Then again, I think of her almost every day.

For so long, it was just the two of us, best of friends.

Any people, any fancy trappings missing from my life, I never noticed.

Besides, just a short bus ride away were the great movie places of downtown. The Chicago, the State, the Roosevelt, the Oriental, the Woods, the United Artists, the Bismarck. We didn't care what was on: kung fu flicks, cheapie horrors, Pam Grier kicking-butt-and-taking-no-names, we saw them all. Still, our all-time favorites were the Technicolor musicals and the classic Hollywood films in black and white. These were only available at the old revival houses, as they were called then. Places that changed the programs three times a week or even daily.

I wonder what Ma would make of the crowds around me today. They look like exiles in need of transport. Maybe the last train out of Paris? "The Nazis wore grey. You wore blue." But instead of toting cardboard suitcases, these are happy refugees, their belongings an assortment of turquoise beach balls, small green rackets, Frisbees, red coolers, and bags piled high with towels of every color. Not forgetting the crowds of small children, still carrying the kind of pails and shovels I remember from my summer days on 12th Street beach. Only in my time, they were made of tin. And Lord help you, if you stepped on a rusty shovel.

For others in the happy mob that makes an obstacle course of the beach this evening, the luggage is composed of little tables, easy chairs, bottles of wine, and wineglasses. I think of this group as the hopeful ones. Happy throng of friends, lost to laughter and good cheer, in the expectation of catching a hint of the 'green flash.' That moment when a last emerald blaze is supposed to mark the coming of dusk.

Myself, I've never seen it, but I don't blame anybody for trying to glimpse it, either. The sun dipping below the horizon, casting a web of golden rays over the waters of the Gulf, is a grand sight.

Today, there seems to be even more of them than usual. Encouraged by the air of happy anticipation in the crowd around me, I follow a well-trod path on the sand to the Naples Pier. Another dandy spot from which to watch the sunset.

***

The air around me vibrates with shouts of laughter when I step onto the pier. As I shake the sand off my feet, right at the entrance, I'm swarmed by a cloud of tiny faces smeared with ice cream from one of the concessions stands nearby. Pairs of lovers of all ages and compositions amble hand in hand, lost to their own private world. Off to one side, a teenager offers to take a group picture for a large family. A commotion makes a large group of people suddenly move towards the end of the pier in concert, like a school of minnows.

Just as I begin to think it's just another sighting of dolphins, a common occurrence, I catch a glimpse of navy uniforms. Standing on tiptoe ahead of me, I can see a stretcher on the dark wood of the walkway. It is then that I finally pay attention to the buzz of conversation around me.

"Some old lady had a heart attack."

"Is she dead?"

"Who knows? I can't see anything from here."

Maneuvering around the crowd, I am struck by an even more distressing sight that propels me forward without really meaning to. A mob of spectators, cell phones in hand, circles the paramedics and a couple of Naples police officers. I've read of people stopping to record accidents for later posting on social media. Who hasn't? But I've never actually witnessed this sort of behavior before.

Equal parts pitying the woman who suffered the heart attack and appalled by the display, I am preparing to turn around and head home when a louder voice rises above the excited hum. "My watch! I dropped my watch! Careful with my watch!" cries a man standing close by the scene of the accident, his phone now dangling from his hand.

A frenzy of movement, again, a shoal of fish changing direction mid-swim, follows the announcement. As the spectators now move towards him, a few gaps appear up ahead. A handful of paramedics still surround two women. As I come nearer, the woman on the floor of the pier, the obvious reason for the 911 call, shakes her head, waving both of her hands at once.

Hovering over her, a second female seems to be pleading with her, to judge by the look on her face. It's obvious the victim is declining the offer of a ride to the hospital from the emergency crew.

Some feeling I can't explain has me approach the two women. Maybe it's seeing how the two of them are now cast aside in the rush of seeking a new thrill. I'd like to think my better nature, however, made me come to the aid of two people in obvious need of help. Even from a distance, I can see the tears on the face of the pleading woman.

In the meantime, the police officers present have turned their attention towards the still-screaming man. A knot of curiosity seekers surrounds him from a safe distance. There is no approaching the man, whose yells, if anything, increase in volume by the second. He continues shouting even as one of the officers reaches out a hand, in a calming gesture, his partner right behind him.

"Don't tell me to take it easy, man! That's no Rolex! That watch is ten years of your pay, easy. It's got to be somewhere around. I didn't move an inch. I actually saw the old broad go down."

As I close the gap between the now-forgotten women, the man's protests continue to reverberate in the warm air. Even closer, it's obvious the lady on the floor — propped on both hands now, still shaking her head — didn't suffer a major accident, never mind a heart attack. Her face, however, is a mess of red welts. She must've hit the floor like a tree axed by a lumberjack. At least she didn't try to cushion the fall with her hands, resulting in a broken wrist. Small blessing, I know.

I want to think my offer of help, on the other hand, is of some comfort. They both seem confused, even as we watch the paramedics pack up and leave. The crowd, meanwhile, has dispersed. From the corner of my eye, I can still see a pair of police surround the owner of the missing watch, a couple of notebooks in hand.

It's all "what now?" looks between us until I decide to invite the two women home. It isn't easy for the injured woman to maneuver her way on the sand despite the brief distance that separates the pier from my house. Equally difficult for her, it seems, is enduring the pointed looks from the beachgoers. In fact, the accident victim appears equal parts embarrassed and hurt.

By the time we make it inside, away from the heat and the curious crowd, she's hanging on to the taller woman's arm. They both seem exhausted and sink with audible sighs on the couches in the living room. I point to the nearest bathroom and leave them to compose themselves while I go in search of cold water and a bag of frozen vegetables.

Like all of us, I'm so used to my surroundings, that I don't even notice the space around me. As I return, however, I braze inwardly for appraising looks that the living room awakens in too many of our visitors. Acres of checkered marble floors and pristine white walls, the whole presided by the sight of the majestic sapphire Gulf through the wide expanse of glass.

This time, I'm happy to see that there is no awkwardness, no pretense, no labored attempts to ignore the room, either. In fact, after proffering a quick, if heartfelt, burst of thanks for the rescue, my unexpected guests turn towards each other, even before introductions are made.

"Don't even think of it!"

"What? What am I thinking?"

"I can actually hear your brain gears turning. She doesn't have any single male friends. And if she does, we're not interested."

"Why, Ollie Howard, take that back immediately! I've only married for love. Every. Single. Time."

"Good for you, *Mrs. Novak*! The Chase Incident, ring a bell?" the taller one adds, seemingly despite herself.

I didn't know what to expect when I gave in to a generous impulse. Silently chuckling—maybe I shouldn't, I know I shouldn't, but I can't help it—I observe the pair. Despite their age, they seem ready to square off, like two little kids in a schoolyard. I wouldn't be surprised if "did so!" "did not!" rang in the air next.

As they continue to splutter at each other, I notice the shorter one is a bit on the pudgy side, like me, but she wears it well. "Natural Botox," I've heard it called. Her hair is in a blonde Dutch-boy cut. She is impeccably dressed in expensive clothes that, even I can tell, are no longer in the latest fashion.

The second woman is tall and rangy. She has removed an old White Sox cap and placed it next to her on the sofa. Now, as if preparing to tackle her opponent, she runs her fingers through her grey hair, which she wears very short and spiky. A small tattoo on her inner right wrist crops up when she raises her hand. An 80s punk princess, then.

I also realize my two visitors are related. There's an air of similarity around the blue eyes and the generous mouths. And the hands. Identical, down to the slight kink on the right index finger, although the shorter one's nails are nicely manicured in a light pink polish. The other woman's are cut straight and blunt.

In all my years in business, I always looked closely at the hands. Mouths lie, but hands will often tell you a lot about their owners.

If I still held any doubts, these two are close cousins or sisters, however, that doubt has been dispelled by their exchange. After a few more whispers between them and a couple of discreet elbow jabs, I finally allow myself a tiny cough. That draws their attention.

I mean to ask after the health of the shorter one, I swear. Or introduce myself. But the phrase, "The Chase Incident?" just dropped from my lips of its own volition.

"Please, we don't talk about it. Too painful," says the injured one, still unnamed, raising her hands while rolling her eyes.

"Too embarrassing. Once more, many thanks," says the other, her good manners apparently recovered. "Thanks for the rescue."

"Yes, oh my word, yes! Ollie is right. What must you be thinking of us? I'm so sorry. Again, I cannot thank you enough for taking me away from that crowd of vultures. I'm Maureen Novak. I don't know what I was thinking, babbling on and on."

Before the second woman can introduce herself, she continues. "This is my sister, Olympia —"

"A name she despises from the sole of her size ten shoes," the sister interrupts. "You would, too, if you were my size. I've heard every awful pun on Olympic heights ever conceived, trust me," she says with feeling. "Call me Ollie. Ollie Howard. I'm a widow, too," she adds, with a side glance at Maureen.

"Are you a fellow Chicagoan?" she inquires then while pointing with her head to one of the side rooms. The space is dim, but you can still make out Manny's sports memorabilia against the white walls of his office.

"Yes, I am," I answer, pointing in turn to her baseball cap. "Go, White Sox. I'm Betty, Betty Manuel. "

"Ahhh, a fellow South Sider."

"Originally, yes. But later, we moved to..." I let my words drop unfinished the very moment it appears, the sisters recognize my last name, both of them at the same time, it seems.

Good manners appear to prevent them from asking for confirming details. But of course, like half the population of the Chicagoland area, they've heard the news. Manny's, originally a brats and fries stand, later a chain of QSRs in the city and the suburbs, was sold for two billion dollars. It's been a year, but few people forget that kind of news item.

"Yeah, that Manuel." I suppose I want to rescue my reputation. Not appear like another rich, idle wife, particularly before Ollie's straightforward gaze. So, I add, almost defiantly. "I was the store's accountant for years. Kept the books for all the first restaurants. Later, I spent many years in Operations. Even when the droves of young MBAs arrived."

"Next thing I know, we're out. Done deal. I wasn't totally happy, but how could I say no to the sale? How could I tell that to Manny, who's worked since he was ten years old?"

I admire extroverts. I really do. Even envy them at times. I'm not a person who's comfortable with spilling my heart out to others, even less on a first meeting. Manny says it takes me about a hundred years to make up my mind about people. And another hundred to act on it.

But there's something in the two faces lifted towards mine, both smiling — one inviting me to let my feelings fly free, the other reassuring me all will be well, no matter what I say — that makes me think, once, just this once, maybe I'll let my heart guide me. And so, I'm not particularly surprised when I open my mouth and hear myself say.

"What do you do with yourself when nobody has a use

for you anymore?"

MO

"You go ahead, Mo. I'll finish washing the pots. I have to say, your face looks much better. It should be all gone by the morning. Well, maybe for that bit right here... Okay, no touching, jeez! Mo... Maureen... Maureen Mauverneen, are you still angry? Please, talk to me."

"You really hurt my feelings. What must Betty think of me? A vulgar gold digger."

"Straight from an MGM musical, that's you. Gold diggers of 1958. Okay, okay, no jokes. Again, I apologize. I'm really, truly sorry, truly. Please, please don't be mad at me."

"Very well. I accept your apology." Life's too short to go about holding grudges, I always say. Although it doesn't hurt to make my sister sweat a little. Plus, I know Ollie's big mouth. Boy, do I know it. Told her a million times, too. Sarcasm is such a negative emotion. Ageing, too.

As I go about the kitchen, I feel a warm body against my legs. "Bertie, darling, careful there. I can't afford another fall tonight. That's better. You know I'm wounded, don't you, my sweetie patootie?"

"Sweet patootie, I ask you. Will you stop with the baby talk? Bert's a warrior! The queens of the Celts went hunting with his ancestors."

"Toot, toot, all aboard the Crazy Train! The queens of the Celts," I scoff, bending down to pat Bertie's head. "You're a sweetie baby, aren't you?"

"But you're right. I better go up. I'm exhausted. No yoga tomorrow for me. I look like a deformed freak."

"Honest, you look better already. All the ice helped. You can barely tell."

"How you lie. But thanks. Yeah, icing it right away did

help. Betty must have a bushel of frozen peas in her freezer, at least, the way she kept bringing them out."

"Yep."

"Speaking of Betty. That house... Did you really take a good look at Betty's house? You know what I was thinking?"

"What were you thinking? Like I can't tell..."

"Ta, ta, ta, no smart remarks. You had a point. Hurtful, yes, but a point. I just never thought of men that way before. But yes, a rich husband would be a way out of our present difficultés financières."

"And I suppose you'd offer yourself up as the sacrifice? All tied up to the beat of the drums, waiting for King Kong to arrive?"

"Well, it's been said I have a passing resemblance to Jessica Lange. The young Jessica Lange."

"I'm gonna let that pass."

"Goes to show you, doesn't it? All that money doesn't seem to have bought Betty happiness."

"Amen to that, sister. Can't feel sorry for her, not that she asked for it. She'll just have to find a new sense of purpose in her old age. We've all had to do it."

"Oh, Ollie, we're not old. We'll never be old. But you're right. Kids up and gone. Husbands, two of them, dying too soon. Who knew life would become so difficult? I thought I'd have it all figured out by the time I was fifty!"

"You know what else I'm thinking?"

"I thought you said you were exhausted. What else are you thinking?"

"I know what you were trying to do before. After dinner, I mean. I can so read your mind, missy. And yes, I agree. Reluctantly, but I agree. The time has come to practice some economy at the dinner table. A slight change to our diet may be even healthier. So, a little bit less butcher-scored pork belly and more cassoulet toulousain, pas d'ingrédients coûteux! Tonight, darling, that's all I can promise."

"Kudos for casseroles. An excellent beginning. That's all I ask for now, a little trimming at the grocery store. While we're at it, what do you say we give regular dog food a try? I don't think Bert needs to dine on poached chicken breasts from the butcher every night, do you? The occasional treat, yes."

"Oh, my poor, poor Bertie. Not the regular kind of dog food, though. Let's start with something a little nicer. So, he can sort of ease into it."

"Deal. Quality food. But still canned."

"Stop with the c-a-n-n-e-d-d-o-g-f-o-o-d talk, darling. You-know-who-over there is all ears."

"Oh, Mo, here, take your ice pack and go to bed. I think the fall definitely scrambled your brain. Love you."

"Love you more."

INTERLUDE #1

Zounds, I have been summoned! Wherefore the writ, I cannot tell. One moment, my hands are grabbing the saddlebow; the next, I have been cast aground on the quaggy garth like a sippet of moldy bread. I am wreathed in a brimstone fug. Nicolas Flamel, thou scurvy dog, are thee behind this spell? A malison on all mages!

Forfend my person, heavens above. Mists continue to swath mine eyes. Wherefore am I bereft of my gallant steed? Where is my equipage? My valiant men-at-arms?

Stand, stand. Be not afeared! Fear is for poltroons. I've found myself in dire straits, afore. At Lincoln, who secured the north gate while the crossbowmen positioned on the nearby rooftops? Who received a battlefield commendation from my Lord Marshall himself?

'Tis but the freak of a poxy mage what finds me in this

demesne, by my troth. Avaunt, ye mists! Hither to the nearest clerk. I am weary and would fain news of this hamlet.

CHAPTER TWO

CARMEN CITRON, NPD

Like the rest of the properties on the block, this place is its own little slice of Florida paradise. Unlike the other mansions around here, however, you can barely see the cottage from the sidewalk, so lush is the garden that fronts it. Come to think of it, I don't know if "garden" is the right word for it, in fact. It's more of a mini rainforest.

Which is nice. So many of the properties in this part of Naples look too big for their lots. Wall-to-wall house. Reminds me of my tía Carmen when she takes off her girdle after her shift at the pharmacy and sits down in a chair with a deep sigh. You almost hold your breath, waiting for the moment when her butt overflows the seat like a tsunami wave.

"You should talk," I tell myself, thinking of my own hips, rapidly expanding as they come under assault by the yummy Florida food.

"What's that, Cintron? Grouper and chips? Already thinking of lunch?" I only shrug in response to Alexander's comment. As we approach the porch, it's time to put my game face on.

A wall of vegetation surrounds us on all sides. The house is a small, two-story building. To the left of the property, two dormers over the garage hint of a small apartment. A tree, like a giant beach umbrella, spreads its branches over practically the whole of the yard. Palms, those I can name, too. Even the shrubs abuela calls elephant ears.

The names for the rest of the green stuff? Ni puta idea. As if by magic, I can hear my mother's protests in my ear. "Carmen Catalina Cintrón Cruz, for *that* we sent you to St. Anne's? So you could talk like that?"

She gets it all in, down to the properly accented ó in my father's surname. Midway through my thirties, and I still get the full Latina mami treatment. Me, a full detective, the pride of relatives far and wide, to hear my mom tell it. "Nuestro orgullo, my joy, my daughter Cici." Yes, in a family tree dripping Carmens, Carmencitas, Carmitas, Carminas, like mangoes in July, I go by Cici.

At work, I went for the middle ground. Ms. Carmen Cintron, newest member of the Criminal Investigation Division of the Naples Police Department. Where I've been welcomed with open arms by the guys. We're all guys, as far as I'm concerned, although feminista to the core. My mami taught me well.

I've also run into a couple of dinosaurs in the force, but that's everywhere. Jersey City has its own crop of racist old dudes who still resist working with a smart Latina. What are you going to do, amirite?

I ring the doorbell again. I can hear a dog growling on the other side of the door, but otherwise, no steps signaling the door will be open any time soon. It's never a good sign when people resist opening the door to a couple of cops. And Alexander and I most definitely look the part, down to the guns holstered on the hip, light jackets tucked behind them. No hot, macho chest holsters for us.

Then again, given our racial composition, it often takes a lot of flashing of IDs through chained doors to convince the citizenry to open their doors, particularly among the elderly, who sometimes take a couple of seconds to respond to even the politest questioning by my partner, Martin Luther Alexander. Yeah, he, too, also got the full name treatment from his pastor parents, I've heard. The Black and Tan, as I call us in private.

***

"Good morning, ma'am. Detective Cintron of the Naples Police Department. My partner, Detective Alexander."

IDs back in the pockets. I know Alexander is moving behind me, opening a pad, whipping out a pen, and disappearing into the background. Prest-o, chang-o. Gone. How can a guy well over six feet tall manage that act? I'm still trying to find out. Maybe it helps that he's one of the most chill guys I've ever met. And that he probably weighs one hundred and twenty pounds, soaking wet. "Ay, pobrecito, seguro no come bien."

I wrestle my thoughts away from my mami's answer to all of the world's problems—lack of good cooking—and concentrate. From the research available at such short notice, I know the owner of the property is one Maureen Novak. After a swift exchange of introductions, I learn the other resident is a Ollie Howard, no volunteering of relationship status.

I can tell they're related, though. I can also tell they've already had some coffee, which is a pity. Catching people before they're caffeinated is a plus. Unfortunately, it's not a good idea to go disturbing folks in fancy neighborhoods too early in the morning. Getting a rise of witnesses, however, works every time.

Despite the introductions, they both continue to stare at us for a few more seconds. And then the shorter one comes back to Earth. "No, ma'am, thanks. I've had my coffee already. What a beautiful dog," I add, closing the gap between us.

I know Alexander likewise shook his head with a polite no. Both women meet me halfway, coming from behind the kitchen counter. "What's its name?"

"*His* name is Bert," answers the taller one. She's

dressed already in what looks like work clothes. Mrs. Novak is wearing what mami calls a mu-mu. A fancy one, but most definitely a mu-mu.

"Beautiful place you have here, Bert. You're one lucky dog. Reminds me of a rain forest called El Yunque."

I think twice about trying to pet the dog. He looks at me with the eyes of that furious old dude whose cigar was taken away suddenly. Churchill, him. *Ooookay.* I move closer to the women, then. "Yes, it sure is a nice house. This whole block is beautiful. And so close to the beach."

"Alexander, will you look at that backyard?" I enthuse, pointing through a slight arch towards the wide door at the back of the wide hallway that splits the house. "Umm, I imagine it's heavenly in the evening, isn't it?

"Me, I'm new here. Still getting used to Naples, still renting. I imagine rents around here are pretty steep, uh? Property taxes high, too. By the way, how are you feeling, Mrs. Novak? That was a nasty fall you took."

At that, the woman in the mu-mu raises her head higher and points to the side of her face. Angry welts cover the cheekbone area on the left, and a nasty scratch decorates her forehead. With a dramatic eye roll, she then shrugs her shoulders.

I pause for a few seconds, letting them continue the conversation I started with my usual we're-all-gabby-chicas-here patented approach. Unlike most old ladies of my acquaintance, however, these two don't take the bait. They remain silent as they continue to stare at the both of us. No need for words: obviously, Alexander and I are an unwelcomed disruption to their morning routine.

"Well, I guess you know why we're here, right?" I finally ask when the silence goes on a bit too long. "No? Turns out you two were in very close proximity to the man whose watch was stolen yesterday. 'A couple of paces behind them,' isn't that what he told us, Detective Alexander?"

"'Practically stepping on their heels,' is how he put it."

"Stolen? But I thought... I mean, he said he dropped it."

"That he did. Right smack in the middle of the pier. So, it didn't go over the side. And the watch is still missing, obviously. Given all that and how quickly the owner noticed it was gone, we now have us a criminal investigation."

"Higher ups, what are you gonna do, right? They don't want the Naples Pier to get a bad reputation," Alexander chimes in helpfully at my back. And then we lapse into silence.

"Well, it was an expensive watch..." These words are eventually, almost regretfully, directed at me by the tall one, who's been giving me dirty looks since we arrived. Closing her mouth firmly, she then regards me with narrowed eyes, her head thrown sideways as if carefully weighing her next statement.

"And how would you know what kind of watch it was, ma'am? I'm so sorry. I don't remember your last name. What a head, right?"

If I thought playing the memory card would help to put her at ease, I'm to be disappointed. If anything, she looks even frostier, as she reminds me. "Howard. Mrs. Howard, if you don't mind. I know because he yelled, 'It's not a Rolex' or something like that," she adds with an audible sniff.

"Isn't there a record somewhere? I remember a couple of very young policemen around him. They are all children in uniform these days."

I let the crack go. She's right. Half the cops in the squad look like they're auditioning for a junior high play. "You have a pretty good memory, ma'am. That's very good. It should be helpful in helping complete the investigation. So, you're strolling down the pier on a nice evening when Mrs. Novak stumbles — what am I saying? You were there. Why don't you ladies give me your side of the story?

"I see, uh uh, I see," I murmur, nodding with what I hope is an encouraging smile, when both women finish what are surprisingly short accounts of the events at the pier. "So, Mrs. Novak is out of it, what with the shock, understandable. Tell you what—Mrs. Howard, would you help me visualize the scene?

"Where were you standing when your sister fell?" I go on, picking up steam.

"How long after the EMTs arrive did the man yell he had lost his watch? Again, were you on the left or the right of your sister? May I ask what were you wearing? Did you have a purse with you? Do you remember seeing anything at all?"

No matter how quickly I fire the questions, Ollie Howard answers them politely but briefly. Even when I repeat a pair of them, I can't get her to deviate in one detail. She could be a lawyer reminding a client: "Don't volunteer anything. Just answer as concisely as possible. And that's that." Never a good sign.

For her part, Mrs. Novak has kept silent during this new exchange. As if sensing the growing frustration of the other woman, however, she moves closer and grabs her hand. Sensing it won't be too long before we're asked to leave, again politely, I decide then to go in for the clinch.

"Well, allow me to suggest another scenario. To jolt your memory, as it were," I say slowly, all the while focusing my eyes on the tall woman in front of me. "A sister's just been hurt. Naturally, a person is confused. There's a crowd closing around, making the situation worse. The noise is becoming too much, what with the sirens and all.

"And then, what's that? There, on the surface of the pier, nearby—again, he was right behind them, correct, Alexander?" I don't expect an answer from Alexander, and I get none. Moving a bit closer but still in a neutral tone, I continue.

"There, very, very close at hand, is a shiny object. The shiny object gets picked up. Stashed in a pocket. Not even thinking about it, in the stress of the moment. Later, at home, we have time to look at it. Man, oh man, this is so embarrassing. Too embarrassing for words.

"It's a watch. It looks like an expensive watch, in fact. The missing 'not a Rolex' watch. Picked up by mistake in a moment of confusion. Would you say that's what happened?"

"That is not the way it happened."

"That's not the way it happened. So how did it happen?

"I see. Well, that's just one scenario," I repeat, when I hear the same description of events as before. "It's always so much smarter to get in front of the story, in my experience."

"I can also tell you the department is not letting go. Naples protects the visitors, right? And there's the watch owner. According to the man, the watch is an Audemars Piguet. **Aa**-duh-maarz-puh-**gway**." I make a big production of reading the brand name twice. "A Royal Oak Offshore Grande, rose gold on a black rubber strap. Pesky thing those rubber straps, I'd imagine, easy to come undone.

"Engraved on the case back—I'm told case back is the correct term—engraved on the back is the date he made his first million, according to the owner. Worth $775,000." I hear Alexander whistle softly behind me. "Yeah, that's a lot of tax payments, I'd say—"

"According to the owner, you keep repeating," jumps in Mrs. Novak then, interrupting my words. She looks just like one of tía Carmen's tiny, foofy terriers.

"How do we know he's telling the truth? How do you know? In fact, how do you know he even had the darn thing on?"

"There you go, Mrs. Novak. Thinking ahead. Turns out he took a selfie, right before the incident happened. It shows him wearing the 'darn thing.'" I almost sketch air quotes. "That very expensive 'darn thing.'

"He provided us a photograph with a time stamp. That watch was most definitely on his wrist in the minutes right before your accident. We have the time of the call from the EMTs' log, and they match.

"And as things stand, he insists it was stolen. And he's got enough clout to get a police investigation. Says the insurance agency won't settle otherwise. Rich people, what are you gonna do?" I intone, with my mildest smile. Nothing but working stiffs over here.

"Well, ladies, here's my card," after a few moments more of silence, I conclude. "If you think of anything we didn't cover, if you remember anything, if there's anything you want to get off your chest..."

I leave the words unfinished as Mrs. Novak and the furious dog escort us to the door.

***

"That was good, Cintron. Excelente trabajo. What? Don't give me that look. Four semesters of Spanish in college. Straight As."

"And Latinos everywhere praise your name, I'm sure," I laugh back at my partner's grin of pride. So, what's your take on the case so far?"

"A crime of opportunity."

"True that. Although with Mr. Not A Rolex, who knows? Brag about that damn watch one time too many, he could've been followed. But then we have these two," I add as Alexander nods by my side. "Elderly, but sharp. Wouldn't be surprised if one of them has issues with kleptomania. Old age can be a trigger. An intelligent woman now feels excluded, overlooked. Wants to prove her independence. 'You're not the boss of me,' that kind of thing.

"Even wanting to act out against family because

they don't make you feel respected. So many seniors are so marginalized these days. It's happening everywhere, even in Latino families."

"In this case, you also have the financial aspect," Alexander responds, putting his shades back on, the essence of cool. "Bet you anything, if we were to dig, we'd find their finances are a mess. Did you take a good look at the place?"

"I hear you. That yard needs major tending, STAT. The garage is way overdue for a new door. And the house? My papi would be all over that roof. These old places can be real money pits. Gimme a brand-new condo every time."

BETTY

I didn't want to seem like a stalker. That awkward girl in high school who always had to be included in everything. Or worse, make them think I expected any gratitude. But I am still concerned. And I did feel a spark there. Good friends are not made. We just recognize them. I've always felt the truth of that.

The day is so beautiful, too. Still balmy enough to be comfortable sitting outside, a soft breeze lifts the waves of the Gulf in little white caps. The summer rains will come later. For now, it's all clear skies, inviting us to head outside, absorb life. Engage with others! At least, for those people lucky enough not to be cursed with a tendency to overthink every human interaction. Sigh.

Still, just after a few moments of further reflection, I pick up my cell phone and dial the number Maureen gave me as we said our goodbyes. As the number rings, I hear Ma's voice in my ear: "Never regret giving in to a generous impulse." And immediately feel surer of myself.

My polite "How are you feeling today? Better, I hope?" is met with another round of thanks from Maureen. Who then proceeds to tell me she is "scarred for life, for life, I tell you." I smile at that bit, not letting amusement creep into my voice. And then Maureen goes on to confide that something, "something unbelievable," happened to them not an hour ago. She won't say another word after that, however. Other than it has to do with the pier. "That means you, dear heart, are part of it, too!"

We agree to meet in the early afternoon. Maureen insists we wait for Ollie to get out of work. It turns out she's a part-time librarian at the downtown branch. I have to say, Ollie does have that look. Tall, capable, unwilling to put up with fools, which was the trademark of all the librarians of my childhood. Then again, I suppose all librarians look tall and capable when we're little.

With Manny still gone, I don't bother with lunch, just an apple, eaten on the run. Not surprisingly, I'm feeling a little hungry as I arrive at the destination chosen by Maureen. It doesn't help that I can smell the savory smells of Italian cooking coming from half a block away. Throngs of tourists still stroll down the sidewalks of Third Street despite the early afternoon heat.

Along with a stretch of Fifth Avenue, a few blocks further north, this section of Third is one of the most popular spots for visitors. Clothing stores of all kinds, art galleries, and a wide variety of restaurants line the street of what not that long ago was a village of Italian fishermen, I've heard it said often.

I'm a few minutes early, so I position myself in a convenient spot of shade by the door. The early breezes of the morning have disappeared. Instead, patches of water dot the sidewalks, remnants of the showers that are obligatory this time of the year. The humidity is nearly unbearable, although it doesn't seem to faze the throng of visitors. I notice many of them are licking gelato cones from one of my favorite ice cream shops down on Third.

Armed with a frosty bottle of water, oodles of sunblock, and a visor, I thought the couple of blocks to Third and Broad would be a snap. Instead, I'm tired and grumpy. I can feel rivers of sweat running down the sides of my face, washing out whatever efforts at make-up I made before leaving the house. If looking like one of Manny's famous brats on the broiler isn't bad enough, I am put to shame the next second by Maureen's arrival.

Calm and composed, not a drop of perspiration on her face, she pulls up on a vintage white three-wheel bicycle, complete with a tan wicker basket, looking as fresh as… what is it they used to say in the old musicals? As fresh as an English rose.

It helps that she is wearing white linen culottes — not plain shorts like mine — under a gauzy tunic, also white. And sporting what can only be described as An Important Item of Apparel. Broad-brimmed, the straw hat has two wide silk ribbons in a shade of blue that matches Maureen's eyes, which are tied with a perky bow under one ear.

It looks like something Scarlett O'Hara would've worn to a picnic. Should such a vulgar activity as bike-riding had ever occurred at Tara. Across from us, a banyan tree as big as a house, dripping Spanish moss, and the steamy puddles add a certain Southern twang to the atmosphere.

Given the hateful associations of the movie, however, I don't say anything. Instead, I only mutter a "nice hat" as she joins me under the porch.

"It does the job, doesn't it?" Maureen answers daintily. "You can barely see the damage," she adds, pointing to a nasty scratch on her forehead. Before the conversation progresses much further, Ollie joins us. She looks as hot and flustered as I feel. She's wearing what are obviously work clothes, although she's added the old White Sox cap to her outfit.

"Sorry I'm late. I stopped at home to leave Coral behind," she says by way of explanation.

"Coral is Ollie's Vespa," Maureen explains at my look of confusion. "She's fond of naming things, aren't you, dear?"

"That aloe by your front door? It's got Fred written all over him," she answers instead, turning towards me. I think she's joking, but I can't tell. I'm beginning to think these two speak a language of their own.

Ollie's next words confirm my suspicion. "Will you look at that? There goes a Blanche," she says, as the sudden blast of a car horn directs our eyes towards the stop sign at the nearby intersection. "An old dude who relies *on the kindness of strangers* not to get killed when he's out on his bikes," she volunteers next. "I'm sure you've seen them. They're all over town. Riding crazy expensive bikes, dressed in biking shorts and jerseys like they're training for the next Tour de France.

"Most Blanches spent years being in charge. They're the sort of guy who still assumes that as he moves forward, others will get out of his way. They don't take to retirement well," Ollie finishes, Maureen nodding sagely by her side.

I have a good laugh at that one. A Blanche would've described my Manny to a T when we first met. Used to bossing everybody around after just getting out of the Navy. Until he learned to listen, to consider, to reflect.

As I follow the sisters into the cafe, I realize the afternoon is too hot for coffee. What possessed Maureen to choose this place? I have no clue, but I keep silent. Before I can suggest going somewhere else, however, the two sisters make a detour. A deluge of pats and "Who's a good girl? Yes, she is!" is showered then on two dogs lying on a sunny spot by the wide glass window, fronting Third.

Not being a dog lover, I hang back. I don't dislike dogs; I just didn't grow up around pets. And I'm usually leery of undisciplined animals, as I am of undisciplined children.

These poodles, however, receive the pats with the cordial-but-distant air I imagine is common to English royalty. As I'm almost about to curtsy, I suddenly hear a loud voice. "The apricot aristocrat is Mish-Mish, and the grey is Dita, short for Maldita because she's a damned mischievous marvel, that one."

"And Mish Mish? What's that?"

"Apricot in Hebrew. What else?"

The explanation comes from the younger of the two people behind the counter. He is one of a couple of middle-aged men, tastefully dressed in coordinating pastel linen shirts. I wish I could get Manny into those. Sigh.

"Welcome to Café Tortoni," he continues. Taking my eyes from the dogs, I realize then the speaker is strikingly handsome. His features are distinguished by a Van Dyke, like something out of an Errol Flynn movie. I also can't help but notice his moustache and beard, as well as his head, match Dita's coat to perfection.

Turns out the specialty of the house is a drink that the older man by the side of the good-looking strangers calls a "blanco y negro." Cold espresso coffee poured over homemade vanilla bean ice cream. The description sounds so delicious. I am already deciding Cafe Tortoni will become my new destination of choice during the Florida summer.

"Have we met?" the younger man says a few seconds later, as I continue to stare at him, my unopened wallet still in my hand. The sisters have not allowed me to pay for my order.

"So sorry. Has anybody ever told you?... You could be the twin of Gilbert Roland. Again, sorry. You probably don't even know who he was. Old Hollywood star."

"As a matter of fact, I do. Well, I know *of* him. Back home, my grandmother would tell me the same thing. She'd show me pictures of the young Gilbert Roland in ancient

Caras y Caretas. Popular magazines," he clarifies. "Her mom probably had saved every single issue ever published."

"As a teen, I even thought I'd change my name. Octavio Roland — it sounds so intriguing, doesn't it? But I knew my father wouldn't approve. Like he didn't approve of so many other things," he finishes with a soft exhalation.

"Never mind that. His loss... His loss he couldn't appreciate the boy you were. The wonderful man you've become," says his companion, a gentle hand on Octavio's wrist. "A loving husband, a great businessman, an amazing uncle."

"Always a dear, Brad. At least, I know he'd approve of Havee and me both continuing the tradition," Octavio counters with a wide smile as he gestures widely around him. "My father, his father before him, all of them head waiters at the Tortoni, the most elegant cafe in all of Buenos Aires."

The brief silence that follows the pronouncement is interrupted as Ollie chimes in. "My husband was named after a movie star, too. Leslie."

OLLIE

"Leslie, Leslie Howard," I clarify then. "His mom was English. She named him after the actor from "The Scarlet Pimpernel." Boy, did I love that one when I was a kid. *They seek him here, they seek him there. Those Frenchies seek him every —*"

"Leslie was your *husband*?" interrupts the one named Brad. Swift looks are exchanged between the men. Granted, it's an unusual name these days, but the two still seem to find much to marvel at. "Her *husband*. When you said Leslie, we assumed..."

"Leslie Howard, yes," I repeat for a third time as he leaves the phrase unfinished. "Everybody called him Jack. Why?"

"We thought… Oh, never mind that. Anything else we can get you ladies?"

One last round of pats at Mish-Mish and Dita, and we retire to one of the side tables. Soon, we're chatting away like old friends. And then the coffees and pastries arrive, and suddenly, it's silence all around the small, round marble-topped table, only punctuated by a chorus of appreciative moans, until Mo finally interrupts the spell.

"I can taste dulce de leche, but what else, what else? Hang on a sec, ladies. Ollie, don't you dare start without me. I just *got* to get the recipe…"

With that, Mo is off and running back to the counter. Betty and I exchange some more small talk then. What else can we do, given my sister's warning?

Turns out Betty and her mother were huge fans of classic Hollywood movies, like many of us who grew up watching TV in the 70s. In fact, I'm still quoting, *Is he in heaven or is he in hell? That demned elusive Pimpernel*, while I pop into my mouth the last of the pastries that sent Mo into a rapture, when I catch Betty staring at my inner wrist.

"My next one will be 'I'm a librarian. I've seen it all.' Tacos as bookmarks. I ask you, who puts a taco inside a book? I'm saving my left wrist for that one. This one translates as 'Why Not?'"

"Cuor non, the motto of le Marquis de Lafayette. He adopted it very early in life," Mo chimes in, having made it back in time to overhear my explanation. I've never understood the smidge of pride in her voice when she says that. It's not like there's such a thing as 'related by tattoo.'

Per usual, Mo's French pronunciation is so exquisite I can tell it takes Betty an instant to realize my sister's talking about the French Revolutionary War hero. "Poor Bert, stuck at home," I continue, glad of an excuse to move the conversation away from my tattoos. Nobody's business what I choose to put on my body.

"We should bring him with us sometime." I point at the two poodles happily lounging on a ray of sunshine pooling on the floor of the cafe. "You wouldn't believe how smart he is. Bert actually learned to open doors by watching another dog do it on YouTube."

"Never mind, Bertie," says Mo. Oh, so *now* she's the impatient one. "Tell Betty our news."

"You didn't tell her anything on the phone this morning?"

"Nope. I thought I'd let you do the honors. It's you they're after. Ollie Howard, the master criminal."

"The master what? Who says you're a criminal?"

"I had just finished getting ready for work," I announce, launching on a description of the two detectives' visit, earlier. I do a fine damn job of the telling, too. Pithy, concise, no essential details left out. "Just the facts, ma'am." Sergeant Friday would've approved of my performance.

A few minutes later, I finish with the only subjective statements I allowed myself. "We were so taken back, as you can imagine. I think we were on our first cup of coffee. Mo was still in her housecoat."

"My Pucci caftan," my sister corrects unhelpfully.

"But I don't understand?" Betty finally answers, stymied like any sensible person would. "The police thinks you staged Maureen's accident? How? I don't get it."

"No clue what they think. But the lead detective, Citron..."

"Citroën?" this bit, again, from Mo.

"Citroën, really, Mo? Citron, no, Cintron, that's it! Detective Cintron suggested a crime of opportunity. We came, we saw, I stole. That's all she'd say. I've a mind to show her up. And the entirety of the Naples Police Department, while I'm at it.

"I'll just have to wait for the next gambit. Wait to see what the insurance company plans to do. In my experience, when it comes to such pricey items, these companies offer a reward. My vast experience with mysteries," I clarify to my audience of two; one of whom, that would be my sister, has allowed her attention to wander, I note.

"Today's news will report that the watch is engraved on the back. I ask you, print the date you made your first million? Tacky, tacky, my friend. But that bit, we knew about that detail even before the media," I clarify, with a pardonably self-satisfied smile.

"What a day you've had, poor Ollie. No wonder you were short with the detectives, from what you say. What were they thinking?"

"I wasn't very happy with the police, even *before* they started lobbying accusations my way," I go on, a statement that brings a look of faint surprise to Betty's face. "As civic minded as the next person, but if they wanted to talk to us, why invade the sanctity of our home early in the morning? Why not ask us to drop by the station? Because they wanted to catch us unawares, maybe even incriminate us, that's why!"

"Ollie, please, don't start. Next, you'll be bringing out your ACLU card," Mo intones, somewhat distractedly by my side.

"I'm not doing any such thing. Besides, whose side are you on?" Mo doesn't answer or react to the jab of my elbow, either. "Mo? Hello, Mo? Still with us?"

MO

As Ollie recounted the details of the detective's visit—which I heard, oh, only a million times before she left for work—I took a discreet couple of glances at the copy of the Naples News that somebody had left behind on a nearby table. The section with the recipes, the advice columns, the comics — the only stuff worth reading — had been a mite too soggy to read after Bertie had taken an unaccountable dislike to that morning's paper.

"Earth to Mo. Come in, Mo," comes next, as Ollie switches to digging my ribs with a pointy finger. I forgo answering and raise the piece of paper before me instead. "Á Toute Á L'Heure Unveils New Menu." I then turn the page towards my sister with a suitably dramatic flourish. The handsome stranger, the young Richard Burton look-alike from the pier, stares back at us under the headline. I read the caption next. "Philippe DeSant, well-known owner of downtown Naples landmark."

Their reactions, I must admit, are not what I expected. I can understand the flat "oh?" from Betty, who probably didn't notice him there in all the commotion, but there's no accounting for the "who's Philippe...Oh, ugh. Him?" from Ollie.

"Yes, him, Ollie. Right on the Naples Pier, remember?"

"Who's Philippe DeSant? Is he the owner of the watch?"

"Hardly. He's just some creep on the loose. Mo attracts them like flies to..."

"No need for vulgarity, dear heart. And I do not attract creeps. Those are admirers. And you do, too. No need to act all high and mighty."

"You're lucky you didn't say 'gentleman callers,' or I'd have to hit you over the head with — with something blunt and handy. And for your information, we don't have admirers at the library. We have engaged patrons."

"Ladies, please. I get it. You both have different opinions on the single men of Florida, but will you —"

"Single? Half the creeps are very much married. And she encourages them."

"I do not! What a thing to say!"

" — but will you please explain what does this guy have to do with the missing watch? I assume he does, right?" Betty finishes, ignoring Ollie's gross accusations. I don't encourage anybody. I can't help being friendly.

"Don't you remember seeing him at the pier? He was standing near us right before she fell. Him and his smarmy smiles."

"No, sorry, I don't. But I was a few steps back. Too busy looking at the people whipping out their phones. Talk about creeps... So, Maureen, you think maybe he saw something? Do you remember where he was before the accident?"

"I don't remember much after, but I do have a faint memory from before. Very faint. Maybe he saw something? That's what the detective Citröen asked us, right, Ollie? To try to remember."

"That was before and after she pretty much accused Ollie of stealing the watch, of course," I concede, stealing a glance at my sister's furious face. For once, Ollie looks like words fail her. "But the police wouldn't know to talk to him, would they?" I continue, leaving my sister to stew as I turn to Betty. "Would they even have his name? Unless they went around asking for witnesses after we left..."

"I wouldn't know, we left together. But I did give the EMTs my name and address. Just in case we had to call them again after we got to my house. You looked wobbly, poor you."

"You know what, Mo? You may be onto something. Sorry about the pokes. I lost my head there for a second. Injustice has that effect on me." Ollie decides to join the conversation just then. She has on what I privately call her Poirot face.

"If detective... Citroën, I ask you. You do know that's a car make, right? Where was I? Oh, yeah, if the detectives didn't get to DeSant yet, perhaps we can sound him out. Gather his impressions, take them back to her. That'll show them!" she announces with great drama. "The police, I mean."

Before she can start babbling about *leetle grey cells*, I jump in. "Who wants the last alphabit? I think that's what Octavio called them." My words seem to take the wind out of Ollie's sails, although I notice she doesn't turn the cookie down when Betty demurs. I must get this recipe from the divine-looking Octavio.

"Ahem...if you don't mind," Betty begins with a discreet cough after a few seconds of Ollie munching.

"You're both correct. No harm in asking, is there? We could do it casually, go for dinner to his place. It might even be fun. If you don't mind me joining you, I mean..."

As we both remain silent, Betty continues, gathering speed. "I know you have to work, Ollie. Let's go early. You know what they say — Naples midnight..."

"Is 9:00 o'clock anywhere else," this time, Ollie and I complete the sentence with a chorus of chortles. Nothing firm is said anymore about visiting the restaurant, however, as we gather all our belongings and get ready to leave. Not before Ollie and I engage in another round of goodbyes to both humans and doggies, of course.

Outside, the humidity is even worse. It's that 3:00-o'clock-Florida-in-the-summer heat that keeps all sane residents indoors when not seeking refuge from the summer rains.

At the door of the Cafe Tortoni, before we go our different ways, Ollie and Betty exchange cell phone numbers. Plans for the three of us to meet again soon are in the air.

"Thanks so much for the coffee and the treats," Betty adds, yet again. "And let me know if you decide to go to DeSant's restaurant. I'd love to join you two if you don't mind. It's so nice, so very nice," she repeats with a faint timid chuckle, as if embarrassed, "to meet new people at our age."

Despite the debilitating humidity, I accompany Ollie on her walk back home. That cap of hers is not only ancient and disgusting, but it also really doesn't do a proper job of keeping the sun away from her complexion. For my part, I'm so glad I wore one of my widest chapeaux, not the cycling helmet Ollie is always insisting I wear. It's enough I must worry about the permanent scarring of my face; I don't need to deal with frizzy hair, also.

***

"Aren't people funny?" I ask eventually, carefully maneuvering the bike between us. "I would have never pegged Betty as a shy person, would you? Or somebody who had trouble making friends. She spent so many years in business. Besides, I sensed a bond, a real connection between us when we met... Was it only yesterday?"

"You would," my sister answers in the lightest of tones. "You have a real gift, Mo, a way of connecting with others that's nothing short of miraculous." Then Ollie goes and spoils it by adding: "Didn't you tell me you felt a growing relationship with a squirrel last week? The one that was trying to talk to you through the window screen?"

We both laugh, Ollie longer than me, that's for sure, but then she goes on. "I think that's true of most people. At any age, most people are reluctant about asking to be included. They hesitate to reach out. Not you, though. You've been blessed by nature with a sunny disposition. There's no dark corners to your soul, Mauverneen."

"Why thank you, darling. That's sweet of you. But back to Betty—you know what I was thinking?"

"I know exactly what you're thinking. And no, we'll have to find another way of approaching DeSant. We're not springing for dinner at the Tutti Frutti--"

"Á Toute Á L'Heure."

"...At the whatevs. Don't try to change the conversation.

When have you known a restaurant on Fifth to be affordable? We're on a budget, remember? We'll just have to find another way to talk to your creepy gentleman caller."

"Oh, you..."

"Back attcha, oh you."

***

After the divine snack at the divine Octavio's place, we're not much hungry that night. I'm settling down with my journals to work on my plans — still secret — when I hear Ollie's voice floating from the sitting room. "Listen to this. *Mrs. Ferrars died on the night of the 16th--17th September — a Thursday.*"

"How many times are you going to re-read those old things?"

"These old things are like a fine wine. A rare vintage that must be savored slowly, letting it sink into your palate."

"*Riiiight*. Before you get too comfy, any luck with that recipe I asked you to Internet me?"

"Google. It's called Google. How many times do I have to tell you? The Internet is a world wide web. Google is a search engine. What was it again?"

"The alphabits we ate at Cafe Tortoni."

"No, sorry, nothing under that name is coming up. You probably misheard."

"Probably. I suppose I'll have to glam it out of Octavio."

"Good luck deploying a charm offensive in that quarter."

"You'd be surprised what I can get away with. Maybe I'll stop by next time you're working. Get Betty to come with me if she's not busy."

"Say hi to the girls for me."

"I sure will."

"Good night, Ollie," I add, not fifteen minutes later. My mind is blocked. I'll have to wait for the morning inspiration. "Sweet dreams of murder and mayhem."

INTERLUDE #2

Egad, this keep is an utter disgrace. Were I the chatelain of this place, the blackguards would find themselves clapped in stocks 'ere long. The perimeter is open to all comers, for one.

Still, the first order of battle is the cleeking of victuals. A scantling of the fare on hand shews it inedible; no better than pannage, acorns fit only for swine. That is some claim from a warrior who accompanied that most puissant of knights, that flower of chivalry, my Lord Marshall, to the lands of the Levant.

Bespeaking of the Crusades — oh, merry, happy times — there is some fustian bruited about a certain Tortoni. I ween a foreign varlet is abroad in these parts. A picaroon as all of his ilk, methinks. A pox on all outlanders!

Alas, no time to tarry over such ruminations. I am esurient and must secure a goodly repast, 'ere I expiry. Zounds, some of the rustics I espy across the moat seem afflicted by a strange madness. An outlandish cavorting, more akin to a St. Vitus dance than the proper greeting of a man of my quality. And the town crier is a proper poltroon.

CHAPTER THREE

MO

"Shanti, shanti, peace." I open my eyes with the last words. In a nearby bush, a black and yellow bird is singing her heart out. Such a marvel, the gift of her song in the stillness of the cool morning. Were it a person, I'd think she had had one Mimosa too many.

Yes, I just know it's a she. And like me, she's thrilled to contemplate this beautiful world of ours.

The sky is a clean slate of greyish blue in a sea of fleecy clouds. Ferns, like lacy fans, swish our backyard lake into tiny waves. The earliest of breezes stir the mystery shrubs that surround our paved patio. And across the water, Maurice, one of the neighboring Corgis, is asleep on the deck, cute heart-shaped butt up in the air.

Today is the day. Today, I send my intentions out into the Universe and wait, hands cupped, ready to receive its blessings.

If this doesn't work, then next week, I'll start to look for real. Although with the only job description in my resume, "Household manager for over 40 years," I don't see any chance of landing a decent job that will help us bridge the gaps in our income. Otherwise, I know Ollie is going to bring up the subject of renting the cottage again. And I can't deal with that. I just can't. No gathering with my babies around the Christmas table? Unthinkable!

"Negativity, negativity, let's banish negativity for today. Right, Bertie? Bertie?"

I find him inside, parked by his bowl, lapping the water like a traveler who's reached a desert oasis. He is quite good at keeping me company most mornings. I sometimes take an unintended tumble, I admit, laughing at his attempts to mimic my downward dog.

"Right, sweetie? Keep those hips high and dangle your head between your shoulders. Mmmm...sublime. I'm telling you, dogs don't know what they're missing. That first cup of coffee of the day...

"Okay, let's get going, shall we? I do wish they'd have other titles for these than 'Business Plans for Dummies.' Who wants to be seen reading a book for dummies?

"Not that I'm planning to let anybody in on my plans yet. This is my idea, mine alone. I'm not even telling your Auntie Ollie yet. Not until I have some concrete plans, that is. She can focus instead on *the clearing of my tarnished name*, as she keeps calling that business about the watch.

"I just can't believe the detectives would consider her a serious suspect, would they? Could she have done something that awful, in fact? Nah. But boy, oh boy, do I know about your auntie's stubbornness. And where it can lead her. Right into the soup. She will not cooperate with detective Citröen, not willingly, she won't.

"Negativity, negativity, for today, let's banish negativity from our surroundings." I crack the spine of the journal I will be using to outline my business plans then. There's nothing like starting a new phase in our lives with a new journal. As exciting as starting a new agenda on January 1st. Like that first cup of morning coffee, total bliss.

"Let's see, Bertie, let's see. Oh, I keep saying that. Sorry, pumpkin. *Create an executive summary*. Okay, pass on that one for now. *Market research*? I suppose a gut feeling it would prove popular with those people in the B-B-Q rentals doesn't count, uh? Not B-B-Q, whatever. So, pass." Pass, pass, and pass on those, too. "Oh, here we go. *Describe company*."

It takes me twenty minutes, a million erasures later, and I'm still no closer to writing a satisfactory description of the venture. Before me there's just a bunch of phrases. "A small, woman-owned business. Culinary instruction by a graduate of the famed Le Cordon Bleu School. Featuring the best of Southwest Florida's seasonal cuisine. Personal on-site chef also available for your vacation stay."

I have a feeling that, in the end, it'll be too wordy, and it still won't say enough, but this will have to do for now. It's a start. Now, let's have it marinate for a while, so to speak, and I'll keep thinking where to fit the les dégustations. Should I just concentrate on that instead? Oh, dear, dear me.

Maybe working in retail would be easier? As if. As if I didn't have weekly proof that dealing with the public is always so difficult. You'd think the clients would be more patient; we're all volunteers.

"Right, Bertie? People can be nasty, especially when you're a lady of a certain age. Wait a sec, here we go! Sorry, baby, so sorry. Yes, yes, mommy knows you need your sleep.

"*Compile an appendix for official documents*. Bertie, we're going to need new folders!"

***

"Bert needs a folder? What for? Boy, are you jumpy today! How much coffee have you had already?"

"Just a cup. Or two. Good morning, Ollie."

"Good morning. I see you're up extra early today."

"Yes. I wanted to get my yoga done before I began journaling. I wish you'd give it some serious thought."

"What makes you think I don't?"

"I don't call pecking away at your computer journaling. I mean connecting, really connecting. Hand to eye, soul to page."

"And while we're at it, buying tons of stickers to decorate the front and back of said journals. Got you," my sister answers, throwing a thumbs up in the air. "Oh, oh, and having a favorite mechanical pencil nobody else can touch."

"That was the one time."

"Uh huh... Tell you what, let me have my first coffee of the day in peace. Later we can do some wrangling over the merits of laptops vs. paper journals. Deal?"

In answer, I simply push the copy of the newspaper across the counter in Ollie's direction. For the next few minutes, only the sound of sipping reigns in the silent kitchen.

I had to wrestle the paper out of Bertie's mouth earlier, but there was no serious damage done. I don't understand why he has taken such a dislike of the paper these past two days. I am deep in the last of the comics of the day, chuckling softly when I hear Ollie clear her throat.

"A $10,000 reward has been offered for information leading to the whereabouts or recovery of the missing item."

"Oh, my, Ollie, you were right! How did you know?"

"I told you, standard operating procedure, even when the property is not priceless. In the case of huge thefts—"

"A million-dollar watch doesn't qualify as a huge theft?"

"Priceless means museum art," Ollie goes on to clarify. "It's not unknown for the reward to work as a form of inducement. An incentive so the thieves will just settle for the reward money instead. Instead of trying to sell the paintings in the black market, for example."

"There were those Turners back in London years ago. Well-known paintings are not that easy to dispose of, you know."

"I imagine. Well, good guessing, dear."

Ollie just smiles mysteriously and looks pointedly to her right. Across the hallway, in the sitting room, piles of books always await in pyramids around her favorite chair. "No guessing, darling. Decades of experience."

After a few more minutes of companionable caffeinating, I pipe up. "Oh, Ollie, let's do it! Let's go to Á Toute Á L'Heure. We have a real reason now that they've offered the reward. Think what we could do around here with that money! Remember how Jack used to say, you've got to spend money to make money?"

"He was talking about refurbishing two flats in Chicago, not spending a reward check we didn't get yet. But I'll agree that with the reward in play, the plot just thickened. Especially as we know something the detectives don't. The name of another potential witness. Take that, Detective Cintron! I'll show you yet!"

"I only said maybe," Ollie adds when I raise a loud cheer that causes Bertie to jump from his bed, startled. "*Maybe* we should consider dinner at the Tutti Frutti as a form of research."

"*Information leading to the whereabouts or recovery,*" she reads again. "What if we pointed the police in the right direction? What if they don't know about DeSant yet? We could split the rewards with him if he saw something. If the watch is ever recovered. If, if, if, so many ifs."

"But if we go, no fancy drinks," she finishes with a pointed look at me.

"Water, no ice, I swear. Oh, Ollie dear, I knew you'd agree. Go make a reservation. I'll call Betty. Make it for four, just in case her husband's back."

OLLIE

Me, I would've taken Coral. A quick zip up Gulf Shore Avenue, and we would've been at the restaurant in a matter of minutes.

Suffice it to say, however, when I suggested hopping on the scooter, Mo gave me that pained look she gets. No words, just a twist of the lips like she's suffering from gas and is too embarrassed to fart. Or I had just proposed we serve Christmas dinner on cardboard plates. Worse, Styrofoam!

Which would totally make sense to me — using disposable, *recyclable* stuff during the holidays — given all the little ones we are lucky enough to have now in the family, but there you have it. Only lace tablecloths and the best Limoges will do for the holidays, according to my sister.

Plus, helmets are not friendly to Mo's hair, I was reminded. That is an argument I usually choose not to engage in. If my sister wants to court brain damage riding around on her bicycle looking like a crazy who-knows-what, it's up to her.

In any case, here we are, sweating like the proverbial pigs as we hoof it down Fifth Avenue instead of pulling up to the restaurant daisy-fresh and on time. There are plenty of free parking lots in downtown Naples, but as usual, they are crazy congested. So sweating is our lot.

Even as the evening clouds lengthen above, only the paltriest of breezes move the canopy of trees around us. On this stretch of town, Fifth Avenue is awash in restaurants. From tiny Thai noodle shops to English teahouses to the fanciest seafood restaurants, the strip has it all. And on the eastern end, close to the parking deck we used today, the best ice cream in town. Gelato, I ask you! Give me a cone of old-fashioned chocolate.

Five blocks of culinary excellence, I'll grant it that.

Although I'm usually not a fan of Fifth during the season. The Season. Too many people, too many cars, too many egos. I once heard a guy berate a hostess outside a fancy joint with the memorable phrase: "Do you know who I am?" "A Blanche, that's who!" I yelled back as Mo dragged me away.

Today, downtown is a smidge less congested than it would be on a regular January evening when it's risk-your-sanity crowded. Still, the street is teeming with visitors determined to enjoy their summer holidays, towing scores of little children, like waddles of noisy ducklings behind them.

It's easy to understand Naples's allure. To the mix of eternal sun and fabulous public beaches, add oodles of bars, shops, and art venues. In fact, within close distance of the Tutti Frutti sits a shady plaza that is the forecourt of a grand theater, dark in June, home to one of the many theater troupes we're lucky to enjoy in the city.

Close by, parallel to Fifth, is another of my favorite spots in this part of town. The leafy respite that is Cambier Park. Tennis courts, free concerts, the Naples Art Institute, and nestled on the side, our community center. The Norris: a hotbed of intrigue and debauchery. At least according to Mo's yoga tales.

Not that I'm one to make fun of my sister's exercise peeps. Well, not much. Coral, in fact, came into my life as the result of a scotched Norris Center love triangle. One offer too many of a lift on Sheldon Cohn's Vespa to one of their classmates, made his wife bring her foot down. Becky Cohn, a great pal of my sister's, insisted that Sheldon sell the scooter. Cheap and quickly. So namaste to you, Amy Martino, the Vixen of the Norris.

"Come on, Mo! Will you hurry up?"

As always, when we are in this section of town, I forge ahead while my sister "window shops." Mo understands "to window shop" as an activity that requires she stop at every other store, it seems, in order to photograph any snazzy outfit that captures her fancy.

Later, she's apt to disappear and come back with a perfect replica of the outfit in question, culled somehow from that Fort Knox of Fashion that is her closet. She swears, almost daily, that she'll go through it "one of these days." And the clothes still occupy two-thirds of the garage, thank the Goddess.

This time, no snark. Had Chase Novak been smart instead of pretty and younger, he would've raided Mo's closet instead of her bank account. Don't believe me? A couple of years ago, she had me sell one of her old purses on an online site. The sale earned enough for us to pay that quarter's property taxes.

But there you have it. If she won't even share the worst of her financial situation with her kids, her closet is her only source of income, given that the business world has little respect for women with the kind of skills my sister commands. More's the pity.

BETTY

"Betty, over here!" I turn at the sound of Ollie's voice and see the sisters approach me, Maureen still a little way behind. "Sorry we're late."

"Not to worry. I'm always early everywhere. Punctuality is an obsession of mine. I've never missed an appointment without a call, either."

Mo finally reaches our side and pants. "We had to leave Granny by the post office. Every other lot was full."

"Let me guess, not your real grandma?" is my answer.

"My car, bright green like a Granny Smith apple," chimes in Mo with a chuckle as she fans herself with an actual lace fan she's produced from her tiny purse.

While we wait to be seated, I steal a couple of discreet glances and revise my first judgments. Not a punk princess, Ollie. Mom would've described her as "mannish." A Kate Hepburn for our century. Like Hepburn, she seems more at home in white linen slacks and a soft cotton shirt rolled at the cuffs.

As for Maureen, her face is showing signs of healing. Only two days since the accident and the redness is gone. On the other hand, it may be the evidence of an expert hand at make-up. I can't tell. What is obvious is she's chosen her outfit with care again. A one-sleeved top in some light, silky navy material, with a wide ruffle running diagonally across the front, worn with fabulous pearl earrings — surely not real? — beautifully tailored white slacks and oh-my-god heeled sandals.

Maureen catches me giving their outfits another couple of glances. What will these two exotic butterflies make of my shift? I don't know. Not my usual style, but the coral, yellow and grey tropical print seemed so attractive back at the store on Third.

"I love my vintage Martin Grant..." she confides then, leaning towards me. She lifts an arm to show me small gussets, discreetly sewn in under the arm opening, "...even if they keep shrinking at the cleaners."

"Shrinking? More like your butt keeps expanding," adds Ollie with a yelp of laughter that attracts smiling glances from the valet stand. "Thank the Goddess for cotton undies by the yard at Wal —"

"Olympia, *ça suffit*," Maureen snaps back, looking like she's about to rap the sisterly knuckles with her fan. "I'll have you know my clothes are really shrinking…"

I leave them to another round of the bickering that seems routine between them — and quite harmless, as I'm also finding out — and turn to the waiter who's approached at a sign from the hostess.

"If you ladies will follow me." He's a slim young man with the build of a tennis player and a familiar air to his olive-skinned features. I give up trying to figure out where I've seen him before as he ushers the three of us to a shady corner of the restaurant patio.

The evening air is sultry. Still, dining outside is a better option than the freezing environments of most Florida restaurants in the summer. We take our seats at a table set in what is almost a little pergola, half-hidden from the street by an exuberant purple bougainvillea. The welcomed swirl of an overhead fan compliments the refreshing sound of a nearby fountain.

"Welcome to Á Toute Á L'Heure. My name is Xavier, and I'll be your waiter today. I will start you ladies with something cool to drink, and then I'll give you the list of specials for the evening. How does that sound?"

I nod as I lower my face with what I hope is an inconspicuous grin. The waiter's pronunciation of Á Toute Á L'Heure is midway between Maureen's fancy rendering of the French name and Ollie's alternative. This morning, she insisted on calling it the Tutti Frutti when she got on the phone, right after Maureen, with a promised "new development in the case of the purloined watch." I'm starting to lose my heart to these two.

"Sounds like a lovely plan, dear heart. By the way, I notice your name tag says Ex-zay-vee-er, but I hear you pronounce it differently," says Maureen, pointing at his chest.

"Ex-zay-vee-er works, too. Hah-vee-EYR is the original, in Spanish."

"Hah-vee-EYR. Oooh, I like the sound of that! It's so nice to know how to pronounce people's names correctly, like their pronouns. At least, that's what my eldest grandchild tells me," Maureen adds, adjusting the ruffle of her top for better

effect. "Well, Hah-vee-EYR, I'll start with a split of champ —
ouch! Never mind, dear. Water, no ice, please."

"Same for me," echoes Ollie, placing both hands then
on the white tablecloth.

"I'll start with water, too. I'll have wine with my meal,
but I like to take it slowly," I confide to my companions as
Xavier turns towards the inside of the restaurant, tucking his
pad in his long black apron pocket.

"Oh, we have nothing against drinking at the beginning,
in the middle, and at the end of a meal. Far from it," Maureen
pipes in energetically. "We're not drinking *tonight*," she
finishes with a side glance at her sister, who continues to stare
innocently at her nails.

***

I know the food industry. Our businesses may be
different, but I recognize a restaurant that uses only top-notch
ingredients. And in this, the Tutti Frutti, as I've taken to call
it myself, is top-notch. Totally worthy of the rave reviews it
has online.

With an obvious French slant, as the name promises, the
cuisine on offer skews Mediterranean. I order bouillabaisse,
and I'm rewarded with seafood so fresh I can close my eyes
and imagine I'm in a beach-side bistro in Marseilles. I overdo
the bread, unable to resist dipping it into the savory saffron-
scented broth, but still, I can't resist ordering dessert.

The chocolate mousse, Xavier informs us, is a surprise.
Lactose-free, the concoction is made without refined sugar,
too. "It has to be tasted to be believed," he insists. He hasn't
steered us wrong tonight. He is both tactful and honest, a rare
combination in a waiter. He was less than enthused about my
first choice, I could tell, but rather than saying anything bad,
after some gentle questioning, he finally came up with the
perfect entrée for me.

So, I do follow his suggestion in this case, too, and

order the mousse. Hardly a sacrifice. It proves so yummy, so rich without being cloying, I order a second one to pass around, insisting the sisters share in it. It's completely gone in a matter of seconds.

"That...was something," Ollie agrees a few seconds later. "Mo, you've got some real competition in the mousse department."

"Couldn't agree more, dear. That's another recipe I've *got* to get my hands on."

While my companions continue oohing and ahhing over the remains of the mousse—I notice Maureen even licks a finger with the last of the chocolate swirl—I signal Xavier discreetly to bring me the bill.

Much fighting ensues, however, when Ollie opens her eyes and sees the credit card receipt before me. "Oh, no, no, no..." she yelps, tugging at the paper. "Not at all. Three ways. There's two of us and one of you!"

"And I ordered two desserts *and* wine. My treat this time. Remember? The Tortoni was your treat!"

"Hardly the same! Absolutely not, Betty. Please, dear, listen to common sense," Maureen insists, adding her credit card to Ollie's, already on the table.

I put an end to the fighting with a flourish to my signature and a shoving of the black folder back at Xavier. "And while you're at it, please open me a bar tab. And bring us a bottle of Veuve Clicquot rosé, please."

Maureen's face lights up at the mention of my favorite champagne. There's an air of resignation to her continuing protests, in fact. Her lips repeat, "No, please, don't," but her eyes say otherwise.

"Please, let me. Let me be extravagant this once. And no more fighting over the bill. Plus, I have ulterior motives." With these words, Maureen's gaze now becomes curious while her sister continues staring sternly ahead.

"Very well, Betty," Ollie finally concedes after a few seconds. "But if you won't let us divide the bill, we won't be able to go out to eat again. I'd be disappointed. Mo would be crushed, I know, but that's my final word on the subject."

"Agreed. From now on, three ways or no way. Unless it's a special occasion, of course."

When the bubbly is finally frothing in the tall flutes before us, I raise my glass. "I did mention ulterior motives, didn't I? I'd like to propose a toast. To catch a thief!"

The movie quote takes the sisters somewhat by surprise, I can tell, so I move in with more energy. "If you're really serious about finding the watch, I'd really like to help. I cannot tell you how good I was about detecting pilfering at work. Another pair of eyes would be useful, wouldn't it?"

"Oh, dear Betty, so sweet of you. You know it was all said in good fun, right?"

"No such thing! Good fun, I ask you. Or have you forgotten? Me picking up shiny things from the floor like I was a superannuated magpie?"

"What a great idea! One for all and all for one, remember that one?" Maureen continues with great dignity, turning to me and ignoring Ollie.

After another few seconds of silence, broken only by the sound of the nearby fountain, Ollie finally unfurls her arms and turns to me. "If you're serious, we'd appreciate your help. And your experience. Of course, we'd split the reward three ways. You did hear there's a substantial reward offered, right?"

I nod, too busy drinking to say more, only to hear Maureen pipe in, lifting her flute. "Here's to us, the smartest cookies around," she adds, a dreamy smile on her face. "Have you ever wondered what kind of cookie you'd be? I'm a pistachio macaroon. I see you, dear Betty, as a yummy, old-fashioned oatmeal."

"You got that right, sister. A nut is what you are," Ollie mutters, rolling her eyes. "One sip of the stuff, and off it goes, straight to her head. Could we concentrate instead on the task at hand?"

"I'd like to propose another toast first, if you don't mind," I continue, hoping I can hold my laughter back. It won't do to spew champagne all over the tablecloth. I meant to hail the official beginning of our partnership. Instead, the words, "Can I be honest...?" drop from my lips before I even raise my glass.

"We expect nothing else from those who would be our friends," Ollie answers, Maureen nodding across me, her eyes still pinched in a gauzy grin.

"On my way home yesterday, I kept thinking about what I said. It's not only that I'm not the most outgoing of persons. Making friends has always been a chore for me.

"It's also that the last year has taught me to be wary," I continue, trying to disguise the disgust I feel at the memories. "The news of the sale of Manny's was out and suddenly, the world seemed a different place. So many pointed looks in my direction when any kind of bill arrives. People claiming to be relatives coming in from under every rock..."

"Say no more! We know people like that. Don't we, Ollie?" Maureen jumps in as I leave the sentence unfinished.

"Every December, without fail, we girls could expect an invite from Da's older sister to Marshall Field's," Ollie goes on to explain. "It took me years to understand why mom would tuck in a couple of twenties in my purse. That was big money for us, too!"

"But there it was, punctual like Field's clock. The check for lunch would come, and Aunt Aggie always happened to have only a hundred-dollar bill on her. We were kids. What did we know? 'You get it this time. I bet you they don't have change for big bills,' she'd always say. Poor mom. Torn between Da's love for his family and Aunt Aggie's ways."

"So, you do get it, then," I say with a sigh of relief. I finally lift my glass then. "To family, freeloaders and all!"

"To the Walnut Room!"

"To the Christmas tree!"

"And the marvy chicken pot pie!"

"To family, the Walnut Room, Christmas trees, chicken pot pies...and to friends who truly understand the meaning of friendship." By the time I proffer the final portion of the toast, I marvel I can remember it all. Another bottle of bubbly arrived at some point and we're hitting it hard.

Soon, we're all deep in the throes of flirting with Xavier. Not my usual conduct, I'll admit, but there you have it. Even Ollie is all in, in a schoolmarmish sort of way. The champagne plus a glass of wine, my usual indulgence at dinner, have truly gone to my head.

However, Xavier is such a good sport, equal parts respectful and funny. All I can do is giggle at Maureen's sass. "My god, Maureen. You can certainly hold your own," I murmur when Xavier is otherwise occupied. "And you're killing it with the fan."

"Practice, dear heart, decades of practice. It's all in the wrist."

"I'm warning you, Betty Manuel, do not encourage her. You'll live to regret it."

Xavier soon returns to photograph our trio while we continue to giggle like a trio of middle-schoolers. For his part, he throws himself into the spirit of the occasion, yelling "Action!" even as he takes several shots, with three different cell phones, from several angles, including a series of retakes, at Ollie's insistence.

I allow myself to sit back on the cool, wrought-iron chair with a deep sigh. And just like that, the thought of making friends causes no anxiety in my usually overthinking brain. What else is in store for me in this new life of mine?

***

Eventually, our laughter grows so loud that when a man approaches our table, I fear it's a fellow diner come to ask us to keep the noise down. The evening air is considerably cooler, and from somewhere comes the scent of a nearby frangipani tree.

"Obviously, Xavi is doing a good job, ladies," he says, as he leans over our table. "Always delighted to see customers enjoying themselves. I'm Philippe DeSant. Welcome to my restaurant."

On the white tablecloth are his hands, not five inches away from me. His wrists are deeply tanned, his fingers long and elegant like a pianist or the claws of a bird of prey. I suddenly flashback to the pair of bald eagles that usually perch on a church steeple on Crayton Road. There's something very sharp — aquiline, that's the word — to Philippe DeSant's profile. A little too matinee handsome for my taste in men.

I give my head a tiny shake. He is obviously an experienced restauranteur, always on the lookout for his staff's performance. I immediately feel better disposed towards him. It is also obvious Maureen does not share my taste in guys. Her flirting changes in tone then. Whereas before, it was all a silly back-and-forth with young Xavier, now it's equal to equal, for the lack of better words.

A few seconds into DeSant's visit to our table, I hear Maureen ask him for the chocolate mousse recipe. I realize then that was her objective all along. Atta girl!

"You're telling me a woman as fascinating as you doesn't believe you must keep *something* back?" I hear DeSant reply with a chuckle.

"Oh, absolutely. Mystery is the very essence of seduction," Maureen answers quickly, sending a swift gaze at him from underneath her lashes. "But pleasure is best when shared, don't you think? And the recipe for that chocolate mousse cries to be shared...with me."

From across the table, I hear a deep groan from Ollie that is lost as Philippe DeSant throws back his head with a roar of laughter.

"Giving in to temptation, my weakest spot. What the heck. If you will follow me, ladies, I'll take you back to the kitchen," he adds with a deep bow.

We follow our host through the courtyard. Beyond the hostess stand is a stained-glass door fitted with massive bronze handles, set in a curved stucco-like frame. A diverse assortment of plaster images — clocks, pomegranates, sirens — surmount the arch. The decorations are so unique that the doorway to Ollie's Tutti Frutti must make it one of the "must-see landmarks" of Fifth Avenue.

***

I am well acquainted with a hot kitchen, deep in the throes of dinner preparation, although as I steal a glance at my watch, I see we're nearing the famed "Naples' midnight." Still, although the main room seemed still busy as we approached our destination, the fact the first dinning rush is over accounts for the brief scenes of inactivity I spy as we enter the long space.

A couple of buspeople stand near an open door in the back, catching a hint of a breeze, water bottles in hand. Through the doorway, I catch a glimpse of a few cars in a rear parking lot under the swaying trees. Soon, our group stops before a stainless-steel counter presided by a short man wearing a colorful handkerchief tied, pirate style, on his bald head and the rubber clogs standard to kitchen staff everywhere. A white tunic strains over a nice-sized belly. Who was it that said, "Never trust a skinny chef?"

"Ladies, meet Naples' best dessert chef. My namesake, Felipe," DeSant's words intrude on my observations. He then gives the beaming man some instructions. "I'll leave you in very capable hands," he finishes, back in our direction.

Despite his words, Philippe DeSant remains close by Maureen's side. Her attention, however, is now completely focused on the man across the counter. Long gone is the batting-eyelashes, flirty woman of a few minutes before.

"Gracias, jefe. It's very simple, really. And best of all, very, what do you call it? Versatile?" I'm pretty sure that's the word, although it comes in three long syllables.

"Always, you need to start with the very best cacao from Oaxaca. Then almond milk, three small, very ripe avocados, or a pound of cooked black beans, up to you. Maple syrup or honey. Me, I prefer raw honey..."

I may not be the gourmand Maureen appears to be—why else would she want the recipe, I now wonder—but I am enough of a cook to be interested in watching a chef at work, so I switch my attention to Felipe's quick hands, as he whisks the ingredients together. Ollie wanders a bit from us but never too far. She obviously gets you cannot get in the way of a busy kitchen staff, particularly by the entrance.

The doors continue to open and close with loud thumps as the demonstration progresses. It doesn't take long, however. As the chef had promised, the dessert is actually very easy to master, so long as you are aware of the so-called secret ingredients. I, for one, would've never guessed he'd use avocadoes, although good Mexican chocolate was always a given.

Felipe, in fact, is nearly done with the dessert demonstration; he has just finished answering a couple of brief queries from Maureen when I sense a presence behind me, a few steps from the kitchen doors.

"Boss, here's that schedule you were missing." Xavier's voice rises above the kitchen din. "It was on the center drawer of your desk, not on the top right, as usual."

Next to Maureen, Philippe DeSant looks up, almost startled. He then studies the paper he is handed the next second, very intently, head down. Next, he seems to come to a quick decision. "Hey, Xavi, I'm going home after this. Will you be able to close? Is your car still at the mechanic's?"

"Yeah, still there. But Anne lent me her baby, her other baby. So, no problem closing tonight. It's right behind us." I turn in time to Xavier gesture with a thumb towards the back of the kitchen, where the door remains open to the night air.

"You and that Mustang of yours. I keep telling you. Get a BMW, a used one. Most reliable cars in the world. Mine has never given me a day's worry."

"When I grow up, I want to be you," Xavi laughs, in reply. "And drive your car." By now, we have all turned to witness the exchange between the two men. Felipe has moved on, his attention claimed by a sous-chef.

"An 8-Series Roadster, top-of-the-line BMW," Xavier clarifies in our direction.

"I drive a Beemer, too," Maureen pipes up happily.

"And yours is thirty years old," Ollie answers. "Hardly in the same class, I'd imagine. I mean, given that grin, that whatever series must be quite the machine."

"'Quite the machine' is correct. Only one of the best German cars ever made, right, boss?" comes Xavier's laughing reply. "Almost indestructible, that kind of engineering. How much did the "Mighty Orange" set you back? A hundred thousand Gs?"

"It's called E-Copper, that color, for your info," DeSant answers with a chuckle, while he dismisses the question of the price with a gesture of his open hand.

Xavier, meanwhile, has turned to the three of us with an even wider smile. "Ladies, I hope you'll visit us again soon. And when you do, don't forget to ask to be seated at my table."

"Thanks, Xavier. And thanks for the retakes."

"Ah, it was nothing, my pleasure. Now, don't go on and forget me, Miss Maureen," he says cheerfully, turning and bowing deeply over her hand. "I expect you to visit me often."

"Will you look at that? You remembered my name, too. What a memory!" says Maureen, with a playful slap at his forearm with the fan she has been deploying like mad in the hot kitchen.

"At his age, we all had memories like that," I sigh back, with a small grin of my own. "It was a pleasure meeting you, too, Xavier. You'll see us again, for sure."

As we approach the swinging doors, Maureen stops, turns, and sends another round of exuberant "thank yous" in the direction of the kitchen staff. Back at his post, Felipe waves back, his smile almost lost in the clouds of steam from a nearby pot.

For his part, DeSant appears strangely subdued. The restaurant business will take it out of you, day in and day out, I'm telling you.

"Yeah, don't worry about it," he yells back, almost curtly, in return to Maureen's continuing gratitude. "Okay, that's that, people. I'm going home now, everybody. Xavi's in charge," he raises his voice with the announcement.

As we exit, the last sound in the kitchen is Xavier's voice, still gleeful. "Yeah, boss, go home. Take it easy. We done good tonight."

CHAPTER FOUR

MO

"So, what did you think? About last night?" I clarify when Ollie only raises an eyebrow in response to my query.

"I'm glad I let you convince me. We made definite progress. Let's give DeSant a day or two, and then we'll think of an excuse to debrief him. But we'll have to do it before Tuesday. The Tutti Frutti will be a madhouse on the Fourth. I just need to come up with a good excuse, a reason why we want to talk to him."

It's as if Ollie can read my mind, I swear. No sooner do I open my lips than she shakes her head and lifts her finger with a stern, "Ah, ah, ah! Don't even think about it! No more dinners."

"Not even a teeny lunch? Oh, you. I'm tempted not to share my idea, then," I continue when she continues giving me that stern look over her reading glasses, ignoring my question. No wonder people think badly of librarians. "I thought I'd go back and ask for permission to use the mousse recipe. I'd wear my clingy Pucci—"

"Nothing doing. I mean, when you go, I'm tagging along."

"Tag along? You don't think I can handle him on my

own?"

"Mo, I think the CIA lost a great agent when you decided to be a housewife. But you'll need me to take notes, won't you? Plus, we can play good cop, bad cop. I'm sure you'll be all too happy to be the good one, too. Lord, woman, you're shameless."

When I don't answer, justifiably miffed, of course, Ollie puts her coffee mug down and turns to me with a wide smile.

"Don't sulk, darling. You're getting frownies. I agree it's a great approach. Brava, Mo."

"And I'll concede, you were right about the place, too," she continues in her most cajoling tones a few seconds later. "Superior food, lovely service. And kudos on the Betty invite. Interesting person, a good conversationalist, and very generous. We'll have to watch out for that distressing generosity of hers, though. I'm not turning into Aunt Aggie at this point in my life."

"Oh, agreed. Interesting and generous and a reminder, once again, that money doesn't buy happiness..."

"...only a better class of misery!" We both finish the quote at the same time, giggling.

"To be fair," I remind Ollie as the sound of laughter dies down in the kitchen, "Betty never said she was miserable. Just lost at this point in her life. And wary of mooches."

"Fair enough, fair enough. Too good a line to pass up, though. What was the name of the vampire duck, by the way? Trey always insisted we watch it every time I babysat him and Molly. There was a nanny in it, too."

"A bigger-than-a-breadbox nanny."

We both continue to laugh for a while, remembering all the hours of watching cartoons with the kids. And then Ollie picks up her coffee and turns to me with a serious look on her face.

"Did that bit about asking DeSant for the recipe come

to you just last night? Just like that?" she adds, snapping her fingers. "I'm impressed. But why do you need permission to use it? In fact, why do you need the recipe at all?" Ollie continues without a pause. "Unless they didn't teach you about avocado mousse — mousses, mices, is that a thing? — at that Pabst Blue Ribbon school you went to."

"Le Cordon Bleu, darling. Will you look at that? Aren't you late for work?" I make a big deal out of checking my watch, hoping to distract her. I am not entirely ready for the turn this conversation has taken, I don't think.

"I start later today. Remember, you packed me lunch. Besides, I need some fresh news, what with Bert deciding we didn't need today's paper. Didn't you, you crazy boy?"

While Ollie continues to pet Bertie, I freshen up both our cups and bring the rest of the muffins to the table. If I had hoped that another blueberry treat would divert Ollie's attention, however, I was sorely mistaken.

"Do you recall that conversation about renting the cottage out for the season? But we're strapped for cash, so who can come up with three month's rent? Weeeeell," I draw out the word as long as I can, "I thought if I could make enough money, we wouldn't have to rent."

"Or if we have to rent," I groan miserably, "I'd have the money for the deposit. I'm telling you, Ollie, it'll kill me." I continue with great energy. "I'll drop dead — dead, do you hear me? I'll collapse right as we close the front door behind us. And what will we do, come Christmas, does not bear thinking..."

"I got you, Meryl Streep. Death, dismay, overall dread, got it. You seem to think I'm jumping for joy at the prospect of commuting to work on a Vespa across eight lanes of snowbird traffic."

"But for now, do please close the conversational loop and don't go off on any tangents. What's your plan to raise money?"

"Cookinglessonswithdegustationstofollow."

"Whoa, whoa. Run that by me again," Ollie chuckles, grabbing yet another muffin.

"I thought," I intone slowly, with a great show of patience, the better to hide my nerves, "that I could offer cooking lessons. Make something of a reputation for myself. And then offer my services as a short-term chef to visitors who don't want to eat out every night. You know, renters who come for a week or more."

"Using local recipes from local restaurants. I'd give the restaurants credit, so it would be a kind of advertising for them. Isn't that a good idea?" As Ollie stares at me, I grab the last muffin and add a nice dollop of lavender-infused blueberry jam for good measure. It is a well-known fact lavender works wonders on upset nerves.

"I even thought that at the end of the lessons, we'd have un dégustation out in the backyard, perhaps," I add, as she continues to look at me in silence, one eyebrow quirked. "Just a small group of people. Bachelorette parties, for example."

I laugh in what I hope is my best "couldn't-care-less" sort of laughter, which still comes out shriller than I'd hoped. Because I realized, even as I spoke, that what I dreaded the most about this conversation was Ollie's feedback.

Not mockery, not really. Ollie's not a mean person. The Queen of Sarcasm that she is — such a vulgar trait, I try to tell her. Ageing, too. But not really mean. Or maybe I say that because I'm so used to her. And I can certainly hold my own.

But as I began the explanation, it dawned on me that I *did* expect some sort of "well, aren't-we-cute?" reaction. I very much suspect that my older sister still thinks of me as a first grader in need of rescue from bullies at Queen of Martyrs.

"Ummm, I don't know about the tastings, but that's a great idea," she finally says, shaking her muffin at me. "Kudos to you. You do have a gift for entertaining. The question is, how do we go about it? How do we publicize it, I mean."

Buoyed by another bite of the muffin—mmm, they're good today—and that "we," I feel a bit surer of myself. "Publicity is not the only thing. I have to come up with a business plan. The recipes must be carefully thought out. Yes, local ingredients, local recipes, but I can't offer dégustations that are going to bankrupt us, for one. One avocado too many in the mousse, and, poof! There goes our profit. So, pricing the lessons just right is just as important."

"Not to mention finding out if there's a way we can have paying guests without a license from the Health Department," Ollie chimes in. "Unless we cheat and have them pay using their phones. But I wouldn't chance it, given how the police are keeping me under surveillance."

"Oh, Ollie. Tell me you don't really believe that," I sigh. With Ollie, you never know.

"I'll tell you what I really believe. I can start today finding out about local health ordinances."

"Oh, darling, would you? That'd be a great help! If only..."

"If only, what?"

"If only we could be ready for the first groups by the end of July? Just a couple of lessons to start. Thank heavens tourists seem to come to Florida every season these days!"

"I'm not sure that's the unalloyed blessing you think it is, but yes, let's aim for the end of July. And then, maybe, with a little cutting back in our budgets, here and there, by the end of November, we could have enough for the deposit for an apartment—"

"If it still makes any sense to move out." My interruption is kind but decisive. "No sense in shrinking our profit margin by paying, in rent, almost what we'll make from renting out the cottage."

"Look at you, talking about profit margins, no less. Maureen Buffet, the sage of Naples."

***

I work some more, fine-tuning the plans after Ollie leaves. Pricing my work as a private chef is giving me the most difficulty thus far. Finally, I put my pencil and journal aside. One of my favorite mantras kept running through my head: "All that I already am is enough." I will figure out the financial side of it, I'm sure.

"Help often comes from the most unexpected sides, doesn't it, baby? Look at Betty, at the right place on the pier, at the right time when I needed her. In the meantime, the universe had responded, Ollie's on board, and now it's only a matter of moving full steam ahead." Bertie doesn't respond to my sally. I find him staring out the back French door, looking as magnificently intent as the lions outside the Art Institute.

And there they are, Maurice and his brother, Chevalier, yapping and running around after a couple of butterflies. Lines of little puffy grey clouds, like little lambs in a row, float above the dogs' sweet furry heads. And the sun, a peeking Little Bo-Peep in search of her lambs, casts its rays on the water.

While the humidity is too awful, even this early, to even think of cracking the windows open and chancing frizzy hair, I stand with Bertie, staring at the sky, deep blue like the clearest of sapphires. Soon, I am lost in daydreams.

Delightful as it is to lose myself in visions of a refurbished cottage, just in time for Christmas, however, if I want us to be able to remain in our home come winter, it is crucial I continue moving my project forward. Now that Ollie is on notice, too, it's vital I show her I can walk the walk, as well as talk the talk, as Brian used to say, bless him.

I must do something, *anything*, today. It is as I place my washed breakfast things next to Ollie's in the rack that I remember. "The Tortoni! The alpha treats! Not today, Bertie, sorry. Mommy is off on a business errand. I swear, I'll take you next time!"

***

I'm in such a "Nine-to-Five" frame of mind that I hum the Parton song under my breath as I drive the couple of blocks to the cafe. Much as I enjoy tooling around in my bike, a totally harmless activity in our neighborhood, despite Ollie's incessant gripes about wearing bike safety—helmet hair, please!—it lacks the necessary gravitas.

And who can even think of talking business while worrying about being bathed in stinky sweat? The red marks on my face are healing nicely—thanks to nightly dabs of EVOO—but I have no intention of arriving dripping concealer and foundation from my face. As if!

The drive also gives me enough time to decide on my approach, particularly as I circle the block several times, looking for parking. The situation requires superior tactics, I'm aware. While most gay men of my acquaintance are outrageous flirts and appreciate a woman putting in an effort with her appearance, I need to make sure my proposal makes business sense to Brad and the divine Octavio. The recipe for the alpha treats, in exchange for publicity for Tortoni.

Soon, however, I'm crossing Third Avenue, a portfolio firmly in hand. It may be that the worrying about the creases on the skirt of my yellow Rive Gauche linen shirtdress—thank God for buttons that can be discreetly moved, is all I have to say—keeps me from paying closer attention, but it's only as I reach the door that I realize the inside of the Cafe Tortoni seems eerily quiet.

Last time we visited, the place was near occupancy. Those ice cream drinks, coupled with their unique pastries, are something else. A second tug at the handle, a quick peek with my hands cupped on both sides of my face—funny, we all do that, even if we've just realized a door is locked—and I can tell the Tortoni is indeed closed, even if the sign at the door says it should be otherwise.

I've turned away when I hear some frantic rapping on the glass. Brad's forehead is scrunched. He's also wearing all black, which doesn't really suit him, pale and silver-haired as he is. Today, in fact, he looks elderly and tired. Still, he gestures energetically with his hand for me to stop. He then ushers me inside and grasps my hand.

"Good! I got you in time. Octavio insisted I open. *Our Tortoni must honor its namesake.* Even the death of some tango singer, whose name I couldn't even *begin* to pronounce, didn't close their doors, he sobbed, my poor darling."

"What? Wait, I'm sorry. I have no idea what you're talking about."

"You don't know? It's all over the news already. "

"I didn't get a chance to read the paper. And we don't own a TV. What's happened?"

"You wouldn't know, anyway. Octavio's nephew, his son, really, is dead. He was killed last night. Xavier was his name. Xavier Bianchi."

"Hah-vee-EYR, the original pronunciation," I murmur stupidly, dread growing inside me. "Not...he's not a waiter, is he?"

"Why, yes, downtown. Do you know him?"

In answer, I only close my eyes. I recall then the grin on an oh-so-young face as Xavi bowed charmingly over my hand. "Don't go on and forget me, Miss Maureen." At that, I feel my knees suddenly wobble. Next thing I know, Brad is holding my elbow and leading me towards a nearby chair.

"Xavi? Xavi's dead? How can he be dead? We just saw him last night," is all I can gasp, in between sips of a glass of water Brad has placed by my hand.

"Then you are some of the last people to see him alive.

He was killed in a hit-and-run accident. "

"Oh, my Lord. No, no, no," is all I can answer, shuddering.

"When he didn't show up at home last night, his wife called the police. But it's true what you see on the shows. The cops don't start looking for a while. Besides, he's young—was young. So, the police suggested he may have stopped after work with friends."

"Turns out there's a taco place, down by Bayshore, where a lot of the young Naples waiters go after work. But it was too late for it to be open. And Anne kept telling them it wasn't like him. To make matters worse..."

"You mean there's more? This is horrible enough..."

"I know," Brad draws nearer and strokes my hand. "I'm sorry, I know I'm babbling. It's just that you're the first person I see today I can talk freely to. Octavio is sedated right now. And Annie won't leave his side."

"No, please, go on. It'll do you good," I answer, with an answering pat on his sleeve.

"You're so right. I love that kid. He was such a feature in all the years of my life with his uncle. I haven't had time to process it yet. Turns out he wasn't found until this morning, which makes it all more of a nightmare."

"You mean he was there, lying for hours? He could've been alive. And they just left him there?" I gasp. "And you say he's married?"

Brad seems ready to continue his catalog of horrors, but he simply nods instead. "That's not the worst of it, but let's just stop, right there. Can I offer you something to drink? Some tea? I know it's hot, but tea is the cure for all ailments, my grandmother used to say."

"Yes, thank you, that sounds lovely. Poor, poor Xavi, so young, so unfair. Silly of me, I know, to say that at our age. But yes, life's not fair."

BETTY

The moment I hear the "coo-AH, coo, coo, coo," followed by the sound of my name, yelled loudly, I sigh and nestle deeper into my cool sheets. It's the call of a happy, mournful dove if such a thing can be said to exist, approaching its nest.

"I didn't hear the RV. Or the garage door..."

"I borrowed Freddy's car and left him to drive it back. I was in a hurry to get back home. How's my girl?" Manny jumps into bed next to me, laughing as he says, "Yeah, I know, I know. No outside clothes."

The next second, the offending pair of khaki shorts fly overhead, to be joined soon by one of the old Manny's t-shirts my husband insists on wearing on informal occasions. I then feel the scratchiness of his beard on my face.

"All the better for having you here. Is that what you want to hear?"

"Yes, I do. Go on, go back to the beginning. Tell me all the ways you missed me."

"Well, for one, the ice maker keeps making weird sounds. Death throes groans, far as I can tell."

"It's probably trying to communicate with the mother ship. Keep going."

"No, you keep going. That feels wonderful. Press a little harder...right there."

"That hip still bothering you?"

"These days, what part doesn't? Just keep going. Now *that* other part of me is just fine. No need to go there."

"Are you sure? Should I stop?"

"I dare you to stop. I double dog dare you..."

***

It is a wonderful thing to wake up from a late morning nap to see a beloved face resting on the next pillow. Even if the mouth on said face is partly open, drooling slightly, and snoring loud enough to wake up the dead, as the saying goes.

I stare at Manny for a few seconds more while he sleeps. His nose is peeling badly. Around his eyes, white rectangles stand out from the deep tan of his face, a shade of brown that continues along the back of his neck and the lower portion of his arms. The man sports a farmer's tan year-round. Not that he cares. Coupled with the salt-and-pepper bristles on his cheeks — nobody in the team bothers shaving when they're on trials — and the hair that my husband insists on having cut at a mall chain, he looks a sorry mess. And I wouldn't have him any other way.

I then jump in the shower and am ready to start my day, finally. By the time I go back into the bedroom, Manny is stirring.

"Lunch in an hour? Outside?"

"Where else? Thanks. I love you."

"Love you, too. Good to have you home."

***

Hunger must've trumped sleep because a shaved-and-showered Manny joins me in the kitchen before I'm midway preparing the sandwiches. He is the master of salads, so as always, I leave him to chop and dice with gusto while I finish putting together our lunch. I leave everything set, so I only have to touch the espresso machine when we're ready for dessert and head outside.

The outside dining area, while shady, offers no protection against the humidity, but with the sea breeze swirling all around, it's comfortable enough. The view, on the other hand, is irresistible. Two windsurfers out in the Gulf seem to be in competition, passing and crossing each other time and time again. Against the turquoise of the sky and the blue green of the sea, the yellows, reds, and vivid oranges of the sails remind me of my favorite box of crayons when I was little.

The expensive one, with sixty-four crayons, including the metallic copper color that I always loved the best. Why did the kids laugh when I once used it to color a drawing of myself? I never understood. I still don't.

***

"There you are. What do you think? Romaine, Capri tomatoes, banana peppers, the hot ones, and cucumbers. Olive oil, balsamic and some fresh basil I found. Should go well with the capicola sammies."

"The fridge seems all right, by the way," Manny adds, setting the bowl on the table.

"You're the sous chef of my dreams. Love salad, hate the scrubbing and the chopping."

"If I had a dollar for every head of lettuce I had to scrub and chop by myself, back when we introduced salads, I would've retired at thirty. Good thing I don't mind. Here's to us," Manny intones next, sitting down and lifting the glass of mango iced tea I had set by his placemat.

"And perdition to our enemies," I gladly toast back, the ice cubes in my glass clicking in agreement.

The next few minutes are just punctuated by contented munching. I ask Manny to bring me up to date on the trials, but he waves it away. "Nothing exciting to report. But we heard of some kid out of Tuscaloosa who seems promising. We think we'll check him out next."

"Not so soon, I hope. You just got here."

"I'm afraid so if we're going to be ready for February. Today, though, I'm all yours. So, go on, what did I miss? What's happening at the Botanical Gardens this week? Are the orchid people really a bunch of witches in disguise?"

"You'd think, right? The way they make them bloom. No, not them. They're a nice bunch of people, gardeners. I guess it's the same with me," I continue, with a quick shrug of shoulders. "Same old, same old. Except, that I finally meet somebody I really like. Two somebodies, sisters. We've gone out twice already."

"The right kind of people, in that case. You wouldn't go out with idiots, not twice."

By the time I'm done telling Manny about Maureen's accident at the pier, the coffee is ready. He brings our cups out to the table while I rummage for some Italian cookies in the cupboards. I really dig for the almond crescents today. I keep them so well hidden when Manny is away I often forget where I put them.

"Espresso cut with...three drops of warm milk," Manny chuckles, making a huge production of serving me. "Go on, you were telling me about meeting them for coffee."

I finish with a description of the wonderful dinner at Ollie's Tutti Frutti. "I can't believe it was just last night. I feel I've known them forever."

"Good for you. I hope I get to meet them soon. And Maureen sounds like she'd give me a chance to practice my smooth moves. *Hey, foxes!*"

"Yeah, right, smooth moves." I almost splutter the coffee at the poor imitation. "But yes, I think you'd like them both a lot. They're so funny, each in her own way. So authentic. So really themselves, if you know what I mean."

"Oh, I do. Believe me, I do. No looking down at *the new money*," Manny's voice drips condescension, mimicking some of the snobbiest people we've met thus far. "Remember that old broad at the country club?"

"What did I say about calling women broads, Manny?"

"I take it back, Betts. You're right. She should be so lucky to be an old broad. She and her *tell me, are you owners or renters?* This from people whose money was made a week before ours."

"Actually, I think Maureen's old Naples. At least, her

husband's family are old timers, at least. Her first one, she's been widowed twice. But, agreed, nothing farther than those attitudes in both of them."

"Then I mean it. I hope I get to meet them soon."

As Manny takes a call from Freddy, who's driving back the RV, I pick up the newspaper. I normally read the newspaper with my morning coffee. I'm shaking my head, wondering how I've managed to reach noon without suffering symptoms of caffeine withdrawal, when a photograph on the front page catches my attention. A familiar face stares at me under the headline: "Hit and run victim identified."

The afternoon suddenly seems to cloud over as I go on to read: "The victim, Xavier Bianchi, 29, of Port Royal, had been reported missing by his wife. His body was found in a parking lot off Fifth Avenue, Naples, early Sunday morning. A resident walking her dogs at daybreak summoned police to the scene.

It is believed the accident that killed Mr. Bianchi occurred at 12:30 a.m. or thereabouts, according to the authorities. That was the last time he was seen by his co-workers as he left a nearby eatery.

The driver of the vehicle that struck Mr. Bianchi neglected to notify law enforcement. The case is being investigated as a criminal hit and run. Those with any knowledge of the accident..."

"What's wrong, Betty? Freddy, gotta call you back," I hear Manny say next as he places the cell phone on the table next to the empty plates. Unable to answer, I hold the newspaper up.

"Is it somebody we know? Somebody you know," he realizes when I keep pointing to Xavier's picture, still silent.

I open my mouth and close it just as suddenly. How do I begin to explain to my husband the brief glimpse we had last night of the world within worlds that is a human being? The giggles that punctuated every one of Xavi's replies to Maureen. The "I-know-something-you-don't" mischief in his eyes when we three agreed the chocolate mousse was exceptional. His good-natured "how's this one?" every time Ollie asked for one more retake.

Instead, I mutter weakly, "He was our waiter just last night."

"Poor dude. So young, too. Hit and run, uh? "

"Yes, a hit and run. Oh, Manny," I whisper, blinking tears back and reaching out for the solid anchor of his hand. "The kids. Call them. Now! Life's full of accidents —"

"Please, Betts, take a deep breath. We'll call them later today, I swear. If we call right now, with you like this, they'll end up upset. And then you'll be upset because *they* are upset. Take a couple of deep, good breaths, okay?"

We sit close together, his arm around me, for a very long time. Manny's warmth, the little sounds he makes as he caresses my shoulder, eventually does the trick, although my hand still shakes as I push the demitasse away.

When I finally raise my head, I can still see one of the windsurfers out on the Gulf. Nothing much has changed in the scene before me. Only a few more umbrellas have gone up on the beach since we sat down to lunch.

A few seconds later, while Manny retreats to the kitchen, taking the dishes and cutlery, I call Maureen. She doesn't answer. Neither does Ollie, whose phone goes to voice mail. I'm still trying to decide what to do next when I hear the doorbell.

"I'll get it!" I yell, cutting across the living room towards the front of the house as the bell rings again.

"Betty, will you get that?" comes Manny's answer, who obviously didn't hear me.

I open the door widely on the third ring, an impatient "just a second!" on my lips that ends in a whisper as I'm greeted by the sight of a hand holding up a badge. A girlish hand that seems to retain the dimples of the very young.

Beyond it, I see a riot of black curls framing a face that looks too young for the official-looking badge she's holding. A few steps behind her stands a young Black man, even younger than her. Like his partner, he's got a badge out and is looking back at me with another of those detached smiles that barely reaches the eyes.

"Can I help you?" I ask, taken back.

"Betty Manuel?"

"Yes, that's me. How can I help you?" It finally dawned on me these two youngsters are here on official business.

I hear Manny's voice calling out again. " Is that you, Freddy? Come right in, dude. You're just in time for lunch."

"Manny, Manny, it isn't Freddy. Get over here. Fast."

OLLIE

As I open my lunchbox, packed with last night's leftovers, I am greeted by delicious aromas rather than the at-times dispiriting sight of my usual peanut butter and banana sandwich. Fantastic-in-its-own-right, an Elvis-approved combo, but a little tiresome, day after day.

Particularly when lunch and a half hour of solitude are the highlight of your working hours.

I adore my profession, don't get me wrong. I love to guide people in their search for their next good read, but sometimes, it gets a little too people-y out there. If I am to retain my sanity when answering phone calls about the author of "that book...the one with the red cover," a period of quiet time is a priority.

I reach into the container with my spork and inhale deeply of the smell of parsley and nutmeg. Mo sure knows her way around a kitchen.

All those times she took careful notes when la Nona carefully revealed her best recipes. All those years of standing by Mom's side by the range. All the weeks of devoted study at that school of hers. All those family dinners and lunches and brunches she's prepared for our family and not one, but two husbands' business acquaintances. All that attention paid to the comfort of others; it shows. The woman can cook.

Because what a lot of people don't get is that under that uber-fashionista, sometimes-giddy exterior of my sister, hides a very capable person. Small wonder, Trey lovingly calls his mother "Mama Bear." I have no doubt that, with a bit of luck, she'll make a success of her cooking venture.

Now, how much faith do I have in our combined ability to publicize and price her scheme? *That* is another story altogether.

"Those look amazing, Ollie. What's for lunch today?" The query comes from my coworker, Rosa, off to one side. Considerate woman, she waited until calm had been restored to my face to speak.

"Totes forgot what they're called, sorry. Small fish footballs? Some fancy French name, I bet. Mo cooks, I eat."

"Lucky you. Arturo's good, but not in her master chef class. His meatloaf is a killer, but that's about it. I wish he'd take some lessons with your sister. "

"As a matter of fact, hubby may be able to do just that soon. I'll keep you posted."

"Do that. Well, it's back to Circulation for me. You want the paper?"

"Please. Bert has decided we don't need to find out what's going on in the world these days."

"Do you have a new delivery person? I bet you anything, they did something to him. Poor Bert."

I wave my thanks to Rosa as I pull today's copy of the Naples Daily News towards me. I have the app on my phone, of course, but like most of my contemporaries, reading the news online just never feels the same. I'll glance at the headlines in the evening if I must, but that's about it.

When our generation goes, they'll have to put the last of the newspapers in a museum.

Today's front page is the usual hodgepodge of idiotic politicians acting even more idiotically than usual, if such a thing is possible. I'm almost done scanning the page when an item on the lower right side catches my attention. "Hit and run victim identified."

A few moments later, I finish my water bottle in one gulp to clear the taste of the suddenly curdled fish as I read the last paragraph. "Those with any knowledge of the accident are encouraged to contact the Collier County Sheriff's Office at 239-252-9300."

I pride myself on my detecting abilities. Not for anything I've been reading crime mysteries for the last fifty years. Better concentrate on finding a way to be useful than on the vision of that young man lying alone on a dark parking lot, mortally wounded.

***

Coral is safely tucked away as I scour the surface of the parking lot behind the Tutti Frutti. Off to the left side, fresh-looking skid marks mar what looks like recently laid asphalt. The signs go up the small curb that surrounds the mass of shrubbery that borders the lot. Half the bushes in that section are badly trampled, and the bark of a young tree shows white against the rest of the brown surface.

"The scene of the crime," I mutter to myself darkly. I miss Bert by my side. I'm willing to bet serious money he would be an ace at this business of sniffing out clues.

Nearby, there is a sad mound of wilting flowers and a wooden cross. Flanking them is a piece of cardboard hastily ripped from what appears to be a produce box. Underneath the sign are a small metal car—a kid's toy—and an almost deflated soccer ball. I snap several pictures of the impromptu memorial site for no reason I can understand. I even photograph the messages: "#bocajuniors #labombonera.

"Junior mouths?" "The candy dish?" Google Translate, that cannot be right. Next to the hashtags, there's a few signatures under the phrase "tus amigex." I get nothing intelligible for that one, either.

As I save the pictures, I notice I have several texts from Mo and even a couple of missed calls from Betty. I can well imagine their attempts to reach me are all about Xavier's accident, so I put my phone away without responding.

Time enough for rehashing of distressing news after I've had the one drink I allow myself each evening. Like the brief respite that is my work lunch, there are days when only a gin and tonic will allow me to end the evening without losing my mind at the state of the world.

"The world is too much with us," I murmur as I strap my helmet in place and kick Coral into action. "Only not in the way you thought, Mr. Wordsworth."

***

I took a long way home in an attempt to temper my disgust. Not that it seems to have worked. Humans are worse than termites, I swear, destroying everything in their path. And some would wonder why I prefer animals. Really, you hurt another person with your car, and you run away?

"Really, you hurt another person with your car, and you run away?" I repeat a few seconds later. Not the most soothing of conversation openers, I'll agree, but there you have it.

Trust my sister to have an adequate response, however. Mo puts the spoon down and comes over to give me a tight hug, which lasts long enough to calm me. Well, that and the gin and tonic she proffers. A large one, too.

"I heard. Wait until I tell you how I heard. But first things first. Are you very hungry? I thought we'd have some soup. Soup and bread, always so comforting, even when it's in the nineties outside."

"Couldn't agree more."

A relaxing hour later, soothed by food I well remember from our childhood, a second G&T firmly in hand—some rules are made to be broken—we retake the news of the day. Which turns out to be even more surprising when Mo tells me of the connection between the owners of Cafe Tortoni and young Xavier.

"So, he's married—was married—and leaves a loving family behind. Can you imagine? Those poor people."

"No, I don't even want to *think* about that. Let alone imagine what Octavio must be feeling. Brad said he raised Xavier. And there's more."

"Oh, dear god. As Miss Parker would say, what fresh hell is at hand?"

"He was found without his wallet or his cell phone. That's why the paper said, *finally identified*. When the police first found the body, they didn't even know who he was. I'd imagine there's not that many missing people in Naples with his description, however, so the cops were able to identify him pretty quick."

"The paper didn't mention anything about missing items."

"No, the police are keeping it back from the public. You know what I think?"

"Way ahead of you, sister. That was no accidental hit-and-run. There was a clear motive. Robbery."

"Exactly. He had a brand-new phone, too. Brad and I agreed it sounds awfully fishy. In fact, he texted me with some more ideas just a few moments before you arrived."

"Wait, you're now texting buddies with Tortoni Brad?"

"Levisohn, Brad Levisohn. He gave me his number, see?" she adds needlessly, showing me her phone screen. She must have a hundred undeleted texts in there. "Poor guy, I was the first person he ran into this morning. He's so distraught. But you know men. They can't or won't admit when they need to talk. *Here, let me give you my number*, I said. *Just in case.*"

"*Just in case*? Good grief, Mo, what else are you thinking is going to happen?" I ask, alarmed.

"Nothing's going to happen. Here, let me start your tea, darling. You're all over the place tonight. It just seemed a neighborly thing to exchange numbers at a time like this," Mo continues from the kitchen, a few paces away.

"Absolutely correct, dear. Don't mind me. Mom would've said the same thing. *We're neighbors. It's good for them to have our number*. Well, you can tell Brad when you text next that Xavier's remembered by his coworkers. On the way home, I stopped to check out the parking lot on Fifth—"

"And didn't check your phone," Mo cuts me off. "I know."

"I saw your texts. Betty's calls, too. But I thought it could wait. I was already on my way home. And it's not like I didn't know what was going on already."

"Well, check in next time. Isn't that what you're always telling me? What if something else had happened?"

"Turns out it wasn't about Xavi. I was trying to let you know that two detectives visited the Manuels. She left me a short voice mail, you, too. If you'd checked your voice mail—"

"The police did what? They interviewed Betty Manuel?" Now, it's my turn to interrupt. I yelp so loudly that Bert comes running into the kitchen, his claws sliding off the wooden floor.

"Good dog, Bert," I say, lowering my voice. Always comforting to have him on patrol. "Why did you let me go on and on about the parking lot?" I continue, turning to Mo. "What did they want? What did she say? Please tell me they didn't tell Betty I'm a suspect!"

"Really, Ollie, you need to calm down. I have no idea what the police said. All I know is what I heard from Betty. A Latina gal and a lanky Black kid. That's all her voicemail said."

Mo sees me reach for my phone and puts her hand on my arm. "I've been trying to get ahold of her since then, but she's not picking up. She did mention Manny is back. We'll have to wait to find out when she's not busy."

"Easy for you to remain calm. For all we know, they're planning to arrest me tomorrow."

"Oh, Ollie, don't be silly. Who's the drama queen, now?"

"Mind the tea, darling," Mo chuckles a bit too smugly for my taste, bringing me a steaming cup of chai next. "There's a good girl. Drink it up, and off you go to bed."

"Oh, no, tell me you aren't!" she yells next, as I move towards the sitting room, teacup carefully balanced in my hand. "Don't tell me you're going back to reading those awful stories, are you? Go to bed!"

"Here you go. Gingersnaps for Ollie," she relents a few moments later, however, placing a couple of treats next to the teacup I've set on my armchair. Feeding the world is my sister's vocation.

"Sweet, but with a nice bite, that's the kind of cookie you are. But don't stay up too late. Remember, murder and mayhem can always wait."

"Shows how much you know, my dear," I riposte back, switching the book before me for one of Christie's. "Well, you do know from cookies. But murder and mayhem can never wait."

"Oh, Ollie, not that again? You must have something

new in that pile of yours, surely? Not just murder, but stale, old murder."

"Soup and bread are your comfort food, Christie's mine."

"Speaking of food, tomorrow, one of us needs to stop by Publix. We're almost out of d-o-g-f-o-o-d."

"I'll do it. It's on sale this week. Two for one."

"Hey, Mo, wait up, don't go. Listen to this. This is why she remains the undisputed queen of crime. *I hesitated with my hand on the door handle*," I begin, only to have Mo turn her back to me with a definite flounce.

"No, you don't. I refuse to hear any more about death today. I'm done here. Don't stay up too much longer. No wonder you drag yourself out of bed in the mornings."

"Yes, Mom…"

"Oh, you. Good night, Ollie.

"Good night, Mo."

INTERLUDE #3

Whilst seeking a provender fit for a belted knight, I have finally engaged with some of the peasants. Afflicted these churls with a rare malady that makes them strangely excitable. And oddly furred. That a battler of my rank is reduced to traffik with the baseborn is not to be endured. But needs must.

One of these has informed me, after some strong language on mine part, that the victualing of this keep is in the care of two dames. It is of a piece with the neglect about me. Strange bourne this, where goodwives rule a castle's cellar by their own fiat, nary a manly cellarer in charge.

Therewith, I shall wend my way and make them a pretty bow. Far from a coxcomb I, but I would confess, I have been the preferred sweeting of many a lady in her bower in my green days. Many a kirtle's ribands came undone beneath these battle-scarred hands.

In the time that it takes to recite a paternoster, nay, less, I shall have gained the esteem of these two beldams.

CHAPTER FIVE

MO

"No, sir, you may not. That item is marked five dollars, agreed. And you *do* have seven dollars on your Ahoy, Mate! Rewards card. But you may *not* have the two dollars back. Really," I finish in my firmest customer-service tone of voice.

There are many reasons to shop thrift. For most of our shoppers, it is a way to stretch a dollar. Several customers have also confided they are decorating a second home with quality furniture at excellent prices. Some of our younger patrons are also very much into recycling and sustainability, they tell me as I check them out.

In my case, I must confess I cannot resist a good fashion bargain. I know I'm not the only one who keeps an eye out for the Saint Johns when they arrive. In fact, at the store, we've all witnessed more than one distressing scene when volunteers — ladies who should know better — battle over one of the knit sets. Hair pulling and name-calling included in one memorable occasion.

Helping a worthy cause is always a plus, too. I always feel so much better patronizing The Pirate's Chest, knowing that the proceeds go towards keeping our seas clean and our manatees safe.

For the gentleman, and I use the term loosely, standing before me, however, still arguing that he's entitled to a two-dollar return on his rewards card while wearing a diamond-encrusted Rolex the size of a dessert plate on his wrist, it is obvious thrift shopping is all about squeezing the last juice out of the bargain orange.

Winning is not everything. It is the only thing, his stance telegraphs to the crowd attracted to the cash register by his insisting bellows.

He is another of those men, Ollie's sworn enemies, unwilling to let go, reluctant to no longer be the one in charge of millions of dollars. Those people who probably account for the swarms of speeding Ferraris, hurling Porsches, and almost-flying Jaguars that plague me any day as I toddled peacefully up Tamiami on my way to one of my many volunteer posts.

My lovely volunteer jobs. Where would we be as a country, I always remind people, without "professional volunteers," as my friend Jill calls us?

I give another pointed look in the direction of his watch, and thankfully, he finally stops the verbal assault. I bag the B-B-Q tongs, wishing I could charge him for the darn bag, and he leaves the store. Looking not the least bit ashamed of himself, I may add. Really, some people take the charitable out of me, fast.

My shift over, I exit the store, still shaking my head over the experience. And send another call out into the universe. "I manifest my project. May it soon find a path forward. But if I *must* go into retail," I add, back in a more down-to-earth frame of mind. "Please, let it be babies' clothes."

"One too many like him, and I'm liable to start stabbing people with grilling implements," I finish in a whisper as I slide the key into the car lock.

It is not noon yet, and the heat comes up from the parking lot in waves. A couple of flowers blooming on a nearby jacaranda tree look as dispirited as I feel right now. Perhaps it is the sight of that ridiculous watch, but as I let Granny's windows down before turning on the air conditioning, long overdue a check-up, I remember Betty's cellphone call.

I had just left a discreet phone message last night. Nobody wants to intrude in family time. Wouldn't you know it? We finally connected just as I was just about to start my stint. Given I was due at the cash register soon, the conversation was brief.

There was not much to report, either. The police asked Betty pretty much the same type of questions they asked of Ollie and Me. A fact that should put Ollie's mind at ease, I should think.

Unless poor Betty—unknowingly, I know—made some comment to the detectives that is liable to have them take a second look at my sister as suspect-in-chief. I better not bring that up with Betty. Or my sister, either. My Ollie does love her drama.

From what Betty also reported, the pair were indeed the same two, young detectives that visited us on... "Monday, Tuesday, today's Thursday," I count out loud as I head south on Tamiami. So much has happened in my life. I cannot believe it's only been four days since the accident at the pier.

***

I check my face in the rear-view mirror and narrowly avoid being catapulted into space by a zooming Land Rover. If a smidge less red, the scratches on my face are still visible. And would be even more obvious were I not doing a masterful job of covering the area with foundation, if I may say so myself.

Not too expert an application today, of course. There was much tut-tutting among my fellow volunteers and an overall agreement that strangers are not as considerate as people once were, except Betty, of course. The recollection of Betty's kindness lifts my spirits enormously, even as the air conditioning splutters and begins to blow hot air.

As if the sudden wash of sweat that instantly bathes my face isn't bad enough, there is the memory of the voicemail on my cell, which showed up as I gathered my things, ready to leave. I don't even want to think what Ollie's reaction will be when I tell her Detective Citroën wants to speak to us again.

"Should I? Maybe I can play dumb-bunny and pretend I never got it." Feeling slightly ashamed that I'm not actually ashamed of myself at the thought, I continue down Ninth and head east on Broad. Almost home.

When I get to Broad, however, I come to a full stop. I look around, spot an empty parking spot a few steps from the Tortoni, and ease into it. Obviously, it is a gift from the Universe for all of the morning's aggravations.

With the Fourth of July just a few days away, the cafe is swarming with visitors. All clamoring, it seems, for one of the ice cream drinks. I feel like a total habituée, as I order one, too. In fact, I only say, "Brad, darling, my usual, please. And calories be damned."

He takes the order with a gossipy "Don't leave yet." The divine Octavio is still missing, but a couple of young people, high schoolers by the looks of them, are now assisting Brad, who today is decked out in shades of creamy pink and grey.

"So much better for your complexion, dear heart," I murmur, when he finally comes by with the order.

"Thanks, I think so, too. By the by, the alfajores are on the house today. Octavio came in, before dawn, and baked up a storm. We have more alfajores than we can sell in a lifetime. Here's some more. Please take them, take them all," he adds, proffering a white paper sack.

"Would you mind sharing the name? Just write it on the bag, darling." I'd looked at the hand-written board before, of course, but didn't find anything resembling the alphabets of my memory.

"A-l-f-a-j-o-r-e-s. How do you pronounce it? I see they're not listed on the menu."

"That's 'cause they're an occasional treat. Octavio makes them when inspiration moves him. As to how to pronounce it, you'll have to ask him. My Spanish is limited to *te quiero mucho.*"

"Teh-kyeh-roh-moo-choh."

"There you go. Ready to say I love you to your next boyfriend. And while we're at it," Brad continues, bringing his head closer to me, obviously determined to leave the customers to his young assistants, "I meant to call you. There will be a memorial for Xavi on Saturday at Á Toute Á L'Heure. Please say you'll come. I just know my poor darling would like for you to be there if he knew you were one of the last people to talk to our boy."

Brad's French accent is impeccable, I note as I nod energetically, thanking him as he goes on to say: "You and your sister, of course. There will be no funeral. He'll be cremated. It'll be just the three of us, four, really. We were lucky we managed to get the crematorium on such short notice. Florida, right?"

"So here I am, making the arrangements," he continues, leaning in with a definite "let's dish" expression, "and Anne gets a call. DeSant with the offer of the place for a memorial. He'd like to give the staff a chance to say goodbye. *It's the least I could do under the circumstances,* he tells her. Can you imagine? Bless the man. Octavio was so moved. Can I count on the both of you, then?"

"Add to the list our friend Betty. You met her, that time we visited the Tortoni the three of us."

"Oh, that's right. The one with good taste in men. Octavio is old Hollywood glamour, isn't he?"

"Too, too divine, that he is. How is he doing?"

"Well, you can imagine. Devastated, as we all are. I only hope the memorial will give him some closure so he can begin healing. And then there's Anne. We'd all have been so looking forward to next month, and now this..."

I begin to ask what is happening next month, but the press of customers prevents any further gossipy asides. The wait staff is sending desperate looks in Brad's direction, that he can't ignore anymore. I thank him once more for the invite and the treats, of course, and leave the cafe, reaching for my phone to call Betty.

As soon as I hit the street, however, the aroma of fish, delicately fried, wafts from the restaurants on Third. Despite the gazillion calories I just consumed, my stomach grumbles loudly. I move to the side, ignoring the smirks of two young clients entering the Tortoni. "Excuse *me*," I send pointedly in their direction.

Do I smell grouper and chips? Do I detect a whiff, a mere hint of cilantro? Fish tacos, perhaps? I am then struck by a brilliant idea. Calling Betty can wait. First order of business, checking the fridge at home.

OLLIE

I'm not a morning person. I'm the first to concede. How can my sister get herself out of bed at dawn and be ready to start her day with an hour of yoga is the proverbial mystery, along the lines of the location of the Holy Grail.

Darn the memory. A dollar deposited in my bank account, for every time I've had to reply, "Actually, sir, that so-called *code* is fiction," and we would both be in the south of France, Mo chattering happily away en français.

Not for me, dawn, I repeat. To linger in bed, followed by several mugs of coffee and newspaper in hand, are my vices of choice. Today, however, I had to settle for the phone app. I am determined to ambush the paper person, even if it means getting up while it is still dark. Perish the thought.

What if Rosa is correct? An evil delivery person would account for Bert's recently developed hatred for the newspaper. Otherwise, I can't imagine what has gotten into him. He's usually the bestest, smartest of dogs.

Fueled by coffee and a scanty reading of the latest political shenanigans, I eventually zip up Gordon Avenue on my way to work. My scooter, clean and shiny, thrums below me. The morning breezes caress my face, and another of Mo's excellent lunches is strapped behind me.

"Hellooooo, Naples! That's what you get, sir, for not looking both ways," I sing out loud to a startled passerby. A right turn on Central, and less than ten minutes from the moment I set out from home, I've reached my destination.

Motorcycling is boss, even if Coral isn't strictly speaking a motorcycle. If I had the money, I'd be tempted to go on one of those Route 66 bike tours. Wouldn't that be something? I can just imagine everybody's faces at work if I came back from one of those, with pictures of me astride a Harley Davidson.

As I cross the library's main floor, a few minutes later, I wave at my colleagues at the circulation desk, set under the clock in the center. I'm reminded, then, of one of Mom's choice sayings: "If wishes were horses, beggars would ride." She always had a way to deflate silly dreams.

At this point in my life, I'd be delighted just to be able to stay in the cottage come winter to celebrate Christmas with Mo, Trey, and Dr. Molly and their tribes. And not wince every time I approach the prescription counter, dreading my share of the co-pay. Fancy cross-country tours on Route 66, please!

As if to highlight the silliness of daydreaming, I am soon deep in the boa-constrictor grip that can be an average workday. I said it before, and I'll say it again. I love most aspects of my job. Assisting somebody in locating another title by a favorite author? I'm your woman. "Never apologize for your reading tastes. Romance is the number one genre out there today," as I've said to many an apologetic reader. Not all of them female, I should add.

Tracing lost material for an interlibrary loan request? Again, look no further. I truly enjoy the search and feel a real thrill when I've managed to zero in on the lost volume; most likely misplaced due to the "kindness" of patrons who would help the staff put books away. That's what those little carts throughout the library are for, people!

Despite the "couldda shouldda been an email" staff meeting I'm forced to attend, it is still a very good day when I enter the staff break room for a late lunch, made all the better when I come face to face with the young Shaggy.

Naturally, Shaggy is not his name. But he does bear an uncanny resemblance to Scooby's best human companion. Human, because I'm not forgetting Scrappy.

The nickname was bestowed on my co-worker by one of our colleagues years ago. A colleague — young and hip — who soon left in search of arugula-greener pastures, no doubt. But the nickname stuck.

Being as he is as easy-going as his cartoon namesake, he is known by all at the library, even some of the patrons, by that sobriQUE, as Mo would no doubt pronounce it. "No T at the end, darling." By now, I think we've all forgotten his birth name.

It is precisely about my sister that I want to speak to young Shaggy, so I am inspired to wave one of the open containers and croon seductively in his direction. "Mo made tiramisu..." I accompany the siren call with a conspiratorial grin and a wink. In a second, he's by my side, pushing a chair in.

"Zoinks!" he whispers, winking back. Shaggy never

disappoints his many fans.

"Can I pick your brain, webmaster?" I ask as I scoop another spoonful of the dessert on a plate.

"You know that's not really my title, right?"

"Well, not officially, no. But you're a digital master. At least, you're among the savviest of geeks of my acquaintance."

Polite child that he is, he doesn't make any remarks about people in my demographic and our uncertain mastery of digital skills. Or maybe it is the mouth full of custard that keeps him from speaking. He just nods agreeably instead.

"If I had a new business I wanted to publicize, where would I go? I mean, where would I go *on the Web*? I'm looking to reach visitors to Naples who come to stay a week or so and want to do something different after a day at the beach. People who are really into food. "

"You mean there's any other kind?" Shaggy says with a grin as he waves my hand away as I try to heap more tiramisu on his plate. "Foodies, got it. Well, there's a ton of platforms that deal in vacation rentals. At least a dozen. And not just the ones most people associate with renting online."

"As far as I can tell, all those platforms offer experience packages where people get to eat with locals. Or learn a craft. Or dance naked with dolphins. Don't write that down, Ollie."

I'm erasing furiously as Shaggy asks, "Do you have a website? That would be the first step. Put up something eye-catching. I can do it for you if you want."

"Would you? That would be fantastic. I can come up with some money for you. I don't want you thinking you have to do it for nothing since we're friends."

"Tell you what. You get your sister to make me a couple of these," he adds, pointing to the almost empty container before him, "and we'll call it even. And I'll give some more thought to publicizing your business, while I'm at it. I'll ask around."

"Actually, it's Mo's business, but yes, that would be great."

"In that case, I volunteer to be her webmaster *and* chief guinea pig. I'll try anything she comes up with. I mean, I assume if your sister is involved, it will result in amazing food, right?"

"That it will. She's thinking of becoming a personal chef, in fact. And doing cooking lessons. She also mentioned food tastings at our house, but I just checked, and that's not happening any time soon. So, yes, a food venture."

"In that case, she should think of blogging her lessons first. A blog would get her name out there. She should also get in touch with local companies that handle the longer rentals. There's a few not far from here, downtown. Does she have an angle, something unique?"

"Florida food and the occasional featuring of local restaurants' dishes, unique ones."

"There you go. It's all about branding. We need to start thinking about the visuals. Your house, for one." When I only raise a mystified eyebrow, he continues, "That house of yours would make for awesome pictures for a web page. Totally vintage Naples."

"Remember that time you had us over for Labor Day? And Tim-the-surfer-dude," that, too, is another of our library co-workers, "arrived in his groovy woody wagon? How we all rushed to take pictures? I think Ayesha took some really good ones."

"Our Ayesha? How do you know? Have you seen them?"

Shaggy's face turns a nice shade of crimson that clashes spectacularly with his orange hair. "Ummm...we're friends," is all he says.

I make a mental note then to keep an eye on the very shy, very quiet, Ayesha in Circulation. An Ayesha and Shaggy romance had not been on my library radar, I must confess. Still, I take pity on his obvious embarrassment.

"So, no flyers up on bulletin boards around town?" I ask, to give him a chance to recover. "Even I am not that old-fashioned to advise *that* to Mo."

"Why not?" Shaggy surprises me by saying, with a shrug. "Particularly church bulletin boards. You'd be surprised how many visitors go to church while they're on vacation. I know my mewmaw always does when she's away."

"But there's also have your online message boards where you can have conversations with others in your line of work. You'd be surprised how generous some people can be, willing to share about their experiences. Everybody loves showing their business smarts. Especially if you're good at it."

"Like you," I answer, whole-heartedly, awed by his generosity.

"Thanks, but I'm easy," he finishes, licking the last of the dessert off the spoon. "Feed me, and I'll follow you home, too. "

***

What's the old saying? "We plan, God laughs." Here I was. Content with a late start, energized by a successful workday, fortified by an excellent lunch, ready to wow Mo with Shaggy's sage advice over another luscious, cost-conscious dinner. At peace with the world, in short, as I gather my belongings out of my locker. And then She laughed.

Which is another way of saying, I feel my knees wobble when I see whose call I've missed. Like any sane human being, my policy is never to phone back a number I don't recognize. Otherwise, you're making a gift of whatever few brain cells you have left to the telemarketing hobgoblins. This one troll, however, has left a voicemail.

"Mrs. Howard, this is Detective Cintron from the Naples Police Department. Remember me?"

"Down to the color of your shoes!" I can't help but yell. It's a good thing all the parking spots by Coral are empty, as the afternoon rains apparently kept library visitors away.

"...remember me?" I hear again as I hit playback. "We are asking for your assistance, yours, and your sister's, at your earliest convenience. Could you please call me so we can arrange a meeting at police headquarters, located at... "

I hit the stop button, more unnerved than I would have credited just a few minutes before. The story of the theft of that ridiculous watch has disappeared from the paper, a fact that also added to my feelings the worst was over. It was a mistake, I now realize, to consider myself safe beyond the long reach of the law.

"Good grief, woman, they were at Betty's only yesterday!" I muse out loud, disturbing the birds in the nearby branches again. The strap of my helmet refuses to buckle. Over my head, a plague of grackles seems to mock my efforts with their cries as the tree branches drip, drip, drip dirty rainwater on my suddenly chilled body.

BETTY

I take several deep breaths. Midafternoon already, and there's no shaking the distress that still lingers in me at the news of the death of young Xavier. I conferenced called with the kids that night, but I'm still haunted by the image of a young man of an age with mine, dying alone on a dark parking lot.

There are so many crazy drivers out there, so much road rage nowadays. So much anger everywhere, period.

I push my desk chair back, open my eyes, and gaze around. The dim coolness of my office begins to work its magic; it takes me somewhere peaceful, somewhere safe.

Nothing but white, white walls, white floors, white furniture. Coolness and serenity.

And enthroned between the two floor-to-ceiling glass windows, with a view of my carefully cultivated bamboo and orchid jungle, Maya's majestic painting. "An ambitious painting," as the Cuban painter described it. "Like a woman who knows her worth, a woman who claims her share of the space."

She would know, of course, she's the artist. All I ever see are huge swaths of mango yellow and guava orange, and papaya green; the colors so alive I feel I can taste them with my eyes. Elemental forces rebounding after the many disasters that plague life. No matter what, life finds a way.

A wash of gold, filtered through the leafy green canopy outside the windows, completes the process. Soon, I am deep into list-making. So calming, so conducive to clearing my head.

There is nothing I can do for Xavier. Given the very decisive manner of the young woman detective who interrogated me, however, I fear Ollie's name will continue to be included among the suspects of the watch theft. Maybe a list of facts, as I remember them, would help?

Poor Ollie. How does one clear one's name of a suspicion like that? And what if word gets out that she was a suspect? Is a police investigation like life? Where mud still clings, even after the nasty gossips have moved on to another juicy item?

"To Catch a Thief." I title the document on my laptop with a small smile, pushing aside memories of Ma and me settling in on our sofa to watch Cary Grant romance Grace Kelly in a swoony seaside locale. Ironic that she never got to see me living in a place this gorgeous, she whose loan backed the original Manny's.

"Focus! Focus!" My words seem to echo in the silence.

The facts place Ollie, Maureen, and I at the pier in Naples on a Sunday afternoon, a week or so before the Fourth of July. The place was unusually crowded even for a summer day, probably because of the approaching holiday.

Was the mob scene that made Maureen fall caused intentionally?

Was this a crime of opportunity? The possibility was mentioned by the detectives who visited me yesterday. What do the police know that would have them think that?

Or could the owner of the watch have been followed by somebody who knew of the value of the piece?

Maureen fell a few seconds after the mob scene started. The accident — scratch that — the aftermath of the accident — was recorded by what seemed like a million cell phones.

Are there any witnesses who have not come forward yet?

For my part, the first sign that something unusual was happening was the loud cries of the crowd.

Was the call for 9-11 intentional, to create confusion? It was obvious Maureen had not suffered a heart attack, despite what I first heard.

By the time I reached the two of them, the crew of an ambulance was already on hand, a couple of patrolmen right behind them.

An instant later, it seems, a man yells he's lost his watch. The recording of the event, too, had distracted him.

At the Tortoni, the next day, I get a recap of the sisters' first interaction with the detectives. Have there been more interviews with the police I haven't heard about?

Both sisters claim they knew about the date engraved on the back of the watch from the police. How soon was that information published in the Naples Daily News?

Ollie suggests a reward will be offered. This, too, comes to pass. How did she know?

Also, while at the Tortoni, Maureen recognizes the owner of the restaurant as another person at the pier that day. Isn't it remarkable how she would remember him among that crowd despite the accident?

Why, then, was there no effort to bring up the theft when we met DeSant at the restaurant? Wasn't talking to DeSant the whole reason to visit the restaurant? Odd that.

The day after our visit, the Naples PD visits me. The lead detective asks many questions about the two sisters, which seemed very pointed, almost accusatory.

"Where was Ollie standing when Maureen fell? Maureen dismissed the EMT ride to the ER. Did it seem that she was really hurt? What did they carry in their hands? What sort of clothing were they wearing?" As if anybody could remember clothing details at that moment. Maureen would.

What were the precise words the owner of the stolen watch yelled upon discovery of the missing watch? Did the words "not a Rolex" actually come out of his mouth? As I told the police, I honestly can't say I remember either way.

As I type that last paragraph, a feeling of dread begins to grow in the pit of my stomach. I was certain making a list would help calm me, but the opposite is happening. As I re-read the bullet points, there is worse to come. What if my desire for new friends in my new life has clouded my judgment? I've known them for less than a week. Would the sisters be capable of such an act?

***

I'm startled nearly out of my chair next by the phone vibrating on the desk. As usual, I forgot I had it on silent mode. I answer it at the last minute, as it threatens to fall off the glass surface. My first words barely make sense. I'm still so disoriented.

It's Maureen with two invitations. The first one comes from somebody called Brad, whom she reminds me is Octavio's husband. He's inviting us to Xavier's memorial ceremony at the restaurant—really, I must remember the name, I can't keep calling it the Tutti Frutti.

We three barely knew the young man, of course, but given the circumstances of our one and only meeting, it seems like a kind gesture. I don't know about them, but I am in desperate need of something—some act of closure. I sincerely hope nobody expects me to say a word.

Then, in a very Maureen manner, I'm beginning to recognize—that is, interspersed with many asides and fond words to the still-unknown Bertie—she invites us for nibbles and drinks at their house tomorrow night.

"Manny? I'm sure he'd like that. Unfortunately, he'll be gone early tomorrow morning. A quick trip this time, I hope. Should be back by the weekend."

"Oh, *quel dommage*! Well, never mind, then it'll be a girls' night. But you tell him I look forward to having him soon for dinner. "

"He'll like that," I chuckle as I accept gladly. I end the conversation, shaking my head. It cannot be, right? It cannot be that I would feel such a spiritual connection to a thief, could I?

***

"*Why not*? Why are you sitting there by yourself, muttering *why not*?"

Speak of the devil. Manny comes into my room then, having finished his usual activities when he's back. These include much mechanical tinkering around the house and the occasional meal with a choice circle of pals. The venue is always a local fast-food place where the coffee is a dollar, refills are plenty, and the talk is of the old days when half of them owned two-thirds of the QSR restaurants in the Midwest. Manny calls it "trade talk." Nothing but gossip, say I.

"Trade talk" today centered on the difficulties of

hiring waiters for the summer. Plus, the constant challenge of keeping experienced chefs during the winter season, when all the white-tablecloth joints in Naples are poaching each other's staff. Although the men are all now retired, they keep their ears tuned into the restaurant business in Southwest Florida. The lunch chat this afternoon eventually veered towards late-night safety downtown and the death of Xavier.

"There's talk that the owner, what's his name?"

"Philippe DeSant."

"Good one! More likely Phil Santino if you ask me. There's talk going around that his place has seen better days. He even revamped his whole menu recently. "

"*Better days*? Are you sure it's him? The restaurant was packed when we were there. And off-season, too."

"I'm just reporting what I heard. The word is he's much given to large gestures."

"Well, there is the memorial he organized for Xavier, almost on the fly," I agree doubtfully. I then go on to describe briefly some of the content of Maureen's phone call just before he arrived.

"There you go. Sounds like the guy leads with his gut. On the other hand, I wouldn't make too much of the gossip. We both know the amount of backstabbing that goes on once a place is successful."

"Don't I?! Mutant chickens with eight wings."

"Brats sold cheap because they were rejects from the factory floor. Remember that one?"

"You just reminded me why there's days when I'm so very glad we got out," I sigh deeply, shaking my head at the memory. Those kinds of lies from a former employee, no less, hurt the most.

"Do you regret selling out?"

"Don't you?"

"I do, yeah. How could I not? It was a lifetime," Manny

concedes. "But it's different for me. Putting together the team keeps me busy all the time. For you, I can't help still thinking that the move was a huge wrench. A bigger wrench than you thought it would be, being in Naples full-time."

"Please, you're killing me. Total hardship, living in paradise. Remember? We talked and talked, and we came to a decision. Together. With the kids gone from Chicago, it was easy. And I was so tired of that big old house. Besides, who's the one who said *I'll go and live by the sea like a mermaid*?"

"I would've built a house on the moon if that's what my mermaid wanted."

"No mermaids on the moon, last time they checked," I quip, still feeling like a young girl at his words, uttered with utmost sincerity.

"Not even in the Sea of Tranquility?"

"I'm warning you, Charles Manuel, don't give me those eyes," I laugh, as I put my hands up.

"Uh-oh, I got the full Charles Manuel treatment. You must be serious."

"I got things to do this afternoon. I called the firm. They squeezed me in today, last of the day. The foundation is back on the table."

"Good for you, Betts. Go get them, tiger!"

I cackle as Manny walks away, still flashing thumbs up in the air.

***

Not an hour later, as I exit the building on Fifth Avenue, I gasp for breath. The day is so muggy that I pause momentarily to clear my fogged-up sunglasses. Across the street, I can see sidewalk tables crowded with diners, unfazed by the heat and the threatening skies. Above our heads, a gathering of black clouds doesn't look promising.

The summer rains that seem to arrive in Naples at 3:00 o'clock, as if an alarm clock had been set, are usually passing showers, a bit of dramatic lightning and thundering, perhaps, and then it's all over. Bathers return to the water—if they even left it—and golfers return to the greens, while waves of humidity begin to rise over the streets like a desert mirage. These clouds, however, seem to herald a late afternoon of unrelenting storms.

I clutch my tote, feeling for my umbrella and hoping I'll make it to the car before the skies unleash another round. It wouldn't be the first time I found myself drenched, holding an inside-out umbrella.

The conference with the financial planners went well. It's too early to announce anything, but it seems this time, the foundation will be set on the right track. Despite the oppressive atmosphere, I feel refreshed. The old Betty Manuel, the long-time operations chief of Manny's, the organizer, the doer is back.

As I hurry down the street, another tropical print snags the corner of my eye. A new wardrobe for a new me, perhaps? I laugh, casting a doubtful look at the sky, about to unleash a torrent on my puny umbrella. The topic reminds me of Maureen's talk of the thrift shop where she volunteers. "A treasure trove, I kid you not!" she almost squealed as she described it.

And with that thought comes the memory of Brad's invitation, via Maureen, just as the rain starts. As I approach Philippe DeSant's place, a gust of hurricane-like wind turns my umbrella inside out. I should've known.

I gain the shelter of the entrance as a familiar face catches my attention. I move forward the better to read the notice that's been taped on the double front doors of the restaurant. The arched frame of the entrance and its stucco carving looms like a Medieval cathedral today. I could swear some of the sirens are smirking.

"Closing for a private function," followed by the date

and time. The sentence underlines a photograph of an even younger Xavier, his happy features captured as he smiled over his shoulder. Underneath, the text reads: "The Toute Á L'Heure family asks your indulgence as we close early Saturday to celebrate the life of Xavier Bianchi. We apologize for any inconvenience."

Raindrops begin to hit my bare shoulders, driven sideways by the wind. The unexpected chill makes me shiver. I thrust my umbrella in a nearby garbage can as I race for my car.

CHAPTER SIX

CARMEN CINTRON, NPD

I must admit, I have a soft spot for older ladies. How could it be otherwise? I suppose it goes back to growing up surrounded by a swarm of aunts. Not to forget my mother's many friends. All of them nominal tías; all of them prominent features of my childhood. As a little girl, I'd yell for help, and a dozen aunts — honorary or otherwise — would come running out.

Even now, I know that if needed, all the tías would show up, some of them wielding a flip-flop. La chancla, the Latina female weapon of choice. I can almost hear my dad chuckling so hard, his double chins wobble. "¡Chico, deja eso! Don't even think of tangling with those women when they're on the warpath."

This is by no means a trait I confess to while on the job. Criminals come in all shapes and sizes. Still, I know I was a bit rough on Mrs. Howard the last time. Getting a rise out of a witness, however, is a strategy that's served me well in the past. Plus, I've come up against so many cases of elderly kleptomania that I feel I could teach a seminar at the Academy.

Still, no use in alienating possible cooperating civilians in a case that's going nowhere fast. Which is why I go out of my way to make them both feel welcome today. I come at them first with offers of coffee. The carafe in my hand is waved away quickly. Who can blame them? Ay, Virgen Santa, that powdered creamer! To quote my niece, Karmen — we're running out of spellings by now — "Let it go! Let it go!"

I then produce two bottles of cold water. Not yet 11:00 in the friggin' morning, and it's already unbearable in here. Even with the air conditioning set on "Jersey Shore in January." The two faces before me glisten. Mrs. Novak began applying a lace hankie to her forehead — still slightly red, I note — the second she sat down.

All those smiley overtures earn me is a couple of sniffs. And a "plastic bottles are destroying our oceans. So, no, thank you," from Ollie Howard.

As no nonsense as the last time I saw her. Still employing an old-fashioned librarian glare with the precision of a laser pointer. Turns out she works at the downtown branch. I literally had to check myself from looking for a pencil stuck in that spiky 'do of hers earlier today. Mrs. Novak, on the other hand, seems a bit more relaxed today. I do notice, though, that once done tidying her make-up, she scotches her chair unnecessarily close to her sister's. As if the comfort of a small hand, offered slyly, was needed.

You'd think they'd been met with rubber hoses and truncheons instead of being ushered into one of the nicer interrogation rooms at the Naples police headquarters. Although I have a feeling that finding herself in the darkest dungeon ever in use would not faze our Ollie one bit.

I'll give her a break. I know police headquarters can be plenty intimidating for most civilians. And given the tone of our last meeting... Well, let's just say I deploy my best, girlish smile — the one that has earned me any number of free passes with the tías.

Charm never hurts when you're about to ask for help without necessarily apologizing for previous misunderstandings.

The niceties of the first few minutes are over with. I move towards the door to dim the lights. I wake up the computer, and immediately, a couple of images appear on the wall behind my visitors. With a start, as if surprised to find themselves still out of handcuffs, the two ladies turn around practically at the same time.

"I assume you recognize the scene, correct?"

"Of course, we do. We both enjoy excellent vision despite our decrepitude." The frosty words hang in the dark office for a few seconds. From the level of snark in the voice, I assume it belongs to Mrs. Howard.

"It's a scene of a crowd at the Naples Pier."

"That it is, ma'am. It turns out a couple of people finally came forward with photos of the moment right after your accident, Mrs. Novak."

"Oh, please tell me I'm not about to see myself splayed out like a filet of beef in front of half the tourists in this town!"

"Not at all. As a matter of fact, I haven't seen one unflattering pic of you," I lie easily. "Ladies, we've asked you in because the Naples police would really appreciate your cooperation."

A cropped section of the photograph fills the screen next. "This was taken from an angle to the left of you two," I explain. I zoom in to the corner in question. Although the resolution is very poor, it's possible to detect a section of a man's torso. One hand holds up a phone as if photographing the scene before him, while the other one hangs down.

To the stranger's left stands a woman, toting a straw bag, which dangles several colorful and very distinct tassels. Her hand is a blur, but it seems to be closest to the man with the mobile. Right between them, a few paces behind, there appears a very grainy image of a pair of dark forearms under a white shirt rolled at the cuffs.

"This is what we're seeing," I go on, after allowing both sisters a few seconds to absorb the image. "As far as we can ascertain, at this point, the watch's gone missing. The owner, you will notice, is holding up his cell phone in his right hand in the photo. Notice his left wrist is already bare. This picture was snapped in the immediate aftermath of the accident.

"We've not been able to locate the woman with the showy purse. If she's the thief, she might be long gone. Maybe not. There are reports of other thefts in the area. There always are. Naples is a magnet for petty crime. And don't get me started on seasoned thieves, all of them landing here during the season.

"Anyway, to the matter at hand," I continue quickly. I couldn't help but notice how the two figures in front of me sat up straighter with those last words.

"From where we stand, the photographic evidence makes the two of you the best possible witnesses of the theft. And when I say 'witnesses,' I realize you had other things in your minds at the moment—"

"So much for picking up shiny things like a magpie." Now, *those* words definitely came from Mrs. Howard.

"But I don't understand, detective. That wasn't what you told us at our house just a few days ago. What made you change your mind?" That eminently sensible disruption comes from Mrs. Novak right before things can get extra crispy between her sister and me.

"As I said, ma'am, we now have many images of the accident. Many images, before and after. None of them show the actual moment of the crime, unfortunately, but they do exculpate you. Both of you," I add, nodding towards Mrs. Howard.

"So now we're working on different scenarios. I'm sure you can appreciate that police investigations often go off in different directions than where they started, right?" I finish cordially but firmly. *Civilians!* Why is it that they think the police are always on the right path, from the beginning of an investigation to the very end?

"Almost a week, and we're no closer to finding other credible witnesses," I continue after a few seconds of silence. I do note the two sisters seem to have settled more comfortably back in their seats.

"The key word here is credible. There's a ton of people coming forward because of the reward. Some of them even witnessed the crime from an astral plane. How about that?" I add with a short laugh.

I turn the lights back on and give them a couple of seconds to blink away before moving in. Just as I thought. The two sisters seem more at ease, but my lame attempt at humor earned me no answering smiles, either. Mrs. Novak, for one, looks definitely put out.

"So, this is where you come in. The owner, as it turns out, has many high-powered friends in Naples. He's a value-added customer, apparently. His pals are all screaming that something be done. He has come up with an idea, too. The man says he'll even pay for it, although we'll have to see how it goes. Will you consent to be hypnotized?"

"Ohhhh, hypnosis! I've always wanted to try that." The answer comes from a beaming Mrs. Novak. Yep, a fan of the stars. I push away the memory of tía Carmina and her devotion to the late, great Walter Mercado.

Mrs. Howard, however, has had time to recover her saltiness. She throws her sister some side-eye while saying icily, "And why exactly should we cooperate with you, detective?"

"Because it's our civic duty, ma'am. We see something, we say something." At that, she looks momentarily abashed, which makes me feel a tiny spark of, I don't know...empathy? Shame at the curtness of my tone? What must it be like to be an intelligent, older woman and be corrected by una niña in a uniform? I have no doubt that's exactly how she sees me. A kid. And smarty pants at that.

With that thought, I mutter softly under my breath. "¡Zángana!" One of these days, I'm going to run into Florida's criminal mastermind, who'll turn out to be in her nineties. And then what?

Still, I soften my tone a bit as I continue. "It's just a suggestion, ma'am. I'm not even saying the hypnosis will work, although I've seen some pretty amazing results back in Jersey. It's just a request."

"Oh, Ollie, let's. Our civic duty *and* hypnosis. Some psychic excitement, perhaps? Think about that!"

With her sister's remark acting as a tonic, apparently, Mrs. Howard is back to true form. Zero to sixty in under a second. "No peasant hovels in your past lives, I bet."

"Very well, detective," she says then, turning towards me with a self-assured air. It is as if she's determined to show me up. Score one for our Ollie!

"I'll agree that doing one's civic duty, whenever possible, is always the best choice. We'll do it, detective Cintrón." She pronounces my last name with an accuracy that would make my papi clap.

I leave them for a second, both heads down, while I step away for a quick phone call. "Would tomorrow work for you both?" I inquire, raising my voice over what sounds like two toddlers squabbling.

"Yes, but only in the morning. We have something in the afternoon."

"It's all set up, then. Thanks so much," I tell them a few minutes later. Maybe there's some hope. Maybe I'll get to close the case.

"They'll call you later today with the time, so the tech will need all your contact info. Again, thanks for your cooperation. I have some days off coming up, so it'll be somebody else with you and the hypnotist.

"And yes, you take care of yourselves, okay? From now, eyes down on the pier, okay, mis amigas?" I finish with an even wider grin.

As the words in Spanish float in the air between us, I see them exchange a quick glance. From the look in their eyes, I can almost guess what's coming next. Three, two, one! Yep, there it is. "Oh, we just love Cuban food!" That's from Maureen Novak.

Funnily enough, after the brief spat with her sister, Mrs. Howard has fallen again into a daze. She is now staring into the distance. Relief has erased the severe lines on her face. She'd be the last to admit it, I know, but there sits one happy camper.

"What's not to like?" I laugh back in agreement. "But I'm not Cuban. I'm Jerseyrican, third generation, from Jersey City," I clarify at her look of confusion. "Puerto Rican. Tons of them in Orlando, not so many around here. And let me tell you. As good as Cuban food, Boricua food is better. Especially my mom's!"

MO

With that last phrase, I perk up. Despite the air conditioning, I've been feeling like a frog at the bottom of a sludgy pond. "Never had any Puerto Rican food. What's it like? Is it hot, like Mexican?"

"Some people add ají picante, hot peppers, but no, it's not hot. It's more like Cuban. Make that, Cuban food is like ours. 'Of one bird, the two wings,' goes a poem about the two islands," the detective smiles proudly. "But we usually eat our rice with red beans, not the Cuban frijoles negros."

"Black beans, right?" I guess, feeling quite the linguist.

Between Octavio's alfajores and the free-jo-lais-nee-gross of detective Citroën, I've decided I'm venturing into Spanish next.

"Like the New Orleans red beans and rice? Lovely dish with a long history." I do so know my American food history.

"Yes and no. No spicy sausages, but yes, close."

I steal a quick glance at Ollie, still strangely silent at my side. It is as if she's been transported into another plane by the information the detective just shared, oh-so-casually. Ollie is no longer a suspect; she is in the clear.

I cross my fingers quickly, hoping this means she won't be ready to leave any time soon. I am determined to make the most of this moment. So, instead of beginning a round of goodbyes, gathering my purse, and dragging this weirdly silent Ollie away, I turn towards the detective.

"If you have a minute, I'd love to hear more about Puerto Rican food," I say with a tiny smile. "Your mom's standards. The ones you like the best."

"**Sahn**-gah-nah. Never mind me, ma'am," the detective sighs as she draws closer. I must say, Detective Citroën appears very approachable this morning. A very nice young lady. Pity about the clothes.

"I'm pretty sure I can get you her recipe of arroz con gandules. There's a restaurant in Immokalee that makes it, but never as good as my mami's."

"Ah-**rrohs**-kohn-gahn-**doo**-lehs. I like the sound of that," I repeat back, my smile widening. Most assuredly, I'm having Ollie check me some library language tapes next. "Arroz, I know, but the rest..."

"Rice with pigeon peas. A lot better than it sounds. Cooked with boneless pork ribs, it'll bring tears to your eyes."

"Please, you're making me hungry," I smile encouragingly. "It would mean a lot to me if you'd share your mom's recipe."

I don't dare remind her of our first meeting. Ollie would kill me. Instead, I do adopt a shameless "you owe us one" expression. After all, according to my old tennis pro, the stunning Lars, young Mr. Ashe often counseled: "Start where you are. Use what you have. Do what you can."

"Okay, let me have your phone, Mrs. Novak. Here it goes," the detective says after a few seconds. "Call me, text me, whatever. I'll make sure you get it."

***

The parking lot outside the police headquarters is an unholy mess of cars driving way too fast, given their location, and worried-looking people under already-threatening cloudy skies.

As noon approaches, the heat is unrelenting. Not a palm frond moves in the swampy air. All these years living here, and I still can't get used to the summers. Not that Chicago is such a little slice of heaven in July, of course.

As Ollie and I approach Granny, I still regain enough of my senses, however, to yelp. "DeSant, we forgot to mention him! Oh, Ollie, how could we? You don't suppose we should go back?" I finish doubtfully, staring back. The building looks as distant as an oasis in a Bugs Bunny cartoon, heat mirages rising from the scorching pavement and all.

"Mo dear, don't stand there gawping like a goldfish. Open up, please," is Ollie's only reply from across the hot metal car top. Gosh, she seems back to normal.

"But yes, that you did. You forgot," she has the nerve to add, once inside the uncertain refuge of the Granny. I don't think the air conditioning will cooperate today, either. This does not bode well for the rest of the summer. Oh, my.

"You totally failed to mention him. Chances are that white shirt and those tanned manly wrists belong to your smarmy Mr. DeSant."

"Oh, Ollie, what a…rhymes with witch. Remember? I

asked for the recipe and done, just like that," I finish, more sharply than I intended, snapping my fingers right under her nose.

Ollie, however, doesn't seem cowed. "You didn't ask, Mo. You positively threw yourself at him. Almost performed the dance of the seven veils. The seven couture veils, if I remember correctly," she chuckles. *Somebody's* in a very good mood, for sure.

"I ask you, how did Miss Marple do it? No senior moments for her," she goes on, as I devote my attention to maneuvering out of the parking space without placing my fingers on the infernal steering wheel.

"Come to think of it, Mo, it's not as bad as it seems, you forgetting to name him," Ollie insists after a few seconds of my keeping a dignified silence. From the corner of my eye, I espy her Poirot face firmly back in place. Ollie and her *leetle grey cells.* As if dealing with the lunchtime traffic on Goodlette-Frank without air conditioning in early July wasn't bad enough.

"Think of it. Now that I'm off the suspect list, we can *really* devote ourselves to the case. This is what I'm going to do. I'll volunteer the bit about DeSant being at the pier *after* the hypnotist. What if it turns out we witnessed the actual moment of the theft and don't remember? Wouldn't that be something? The reward would be all ours, then! It won't matter then that you forgot."

That's it, dignity be damned. "I forgot? I forgot?" I repeat indignantly. Or as indignantly as I can while dodging speeding bullets disguised as cars.

In response, she extends her hand to pat mine and adds, in a conciliatory tone. "What happened to 'no frownies'? Think, Mo, a session with the hypnotist. Who knows what the tomorrow may bring?"

"I'm not a child, Ollie Howard," I answer with as

much poise as I can muster, removing my sweaty arm from her grasp. "And don't pretend you care, either. What was that crack about peasant hovels?"

"You have to admit it's strange, my dear. Have you ever heard of one person, just one, who remembers being a peasant in a past life?"

I sniff once, twice, and then complete the rest of the drive home in an icy silence. I swear I don't even feel the heat the rest of the way.

OLLIE

One thing about my sister. She is not one to sulk for very long. By the time we arrive back home, she is Chatty Cathy again. To be totally honest, we both are. Talkative enough to raise the proverbial dead. Or any spirits unwise enough to hang around the cottage. I bet anything there are plenty of ghosts and the occasional banshee watching in these hundred-year-old walls.

I don't share that bit with Mo, though. No need for one of her "I'm an old soul" speeches, as I'm about to expire from hunger. She is now recovered from her funk and is busily rooting around in the fridge. Given our recently adopted regimen, lunch is tasty but nothing fancy.

I take that back. Fancy, but cost-conscious. Turns out she can make those little fishy footballs with canned tuna, too, although she never stops complaining. The original martyr in the Roman Coliseum, my sister. All that whining; wait until she finds out that some more budget cuts are about to go into effect.

A more economical brand of canned dog food—sorry, Bert, my boy—switching to cheaper booze, along with a bare-bones phone plan that goes into effect next month. Fingers crossed, no unexpected repairs, and our combined cottage account should finish the month in the black. Just barely.

But how long can we keep it up? Fact is, there's simply no more fat to be cut, so fingers crossed we can come up with something in the weeks ahead.

Otherwise, it'll soon be time to get in touch with the real estate companies about putting the cottage on the market for the season. Perish the thought. The thought of strangers sleeping in my bed makes me queasy. As for Mo, I don't want to think what she'll make of strangers using the toilets. For somebody who routinely throws herself all over the floor during a yoga session, my sister can be mighty squeamish.

Still, other than the occasional grumble about groceries, I must say Mo is adapting herself to our new life like a trooper. For one, she's gone full-little-engine-that-could with her business venture.

Thank the Goddess, there will be no groups of hungry, nosey parkers showing up at the cottage. The Florida Department of Health will not allow running an unlicensed eating establishment. Wise of them. On the other hand, if you want to hire yourself out as a chef and there are people willing to hire you, "Hey, it's all good" seems to be the prevailing state wisdom.

We have given Mo's cooking business a month to succeed. After that, it's off to the job market for her. Therefore, no sooner do we finish eating than Mo picks up her phone with a decisive air and begins calling local vacation rental companies. At this point, she's inquiring how to get on the list of "local experiences" that Shaggy suggested. "Eat like a local," that sort of thing.

As I go about tidying the kitchen, I see her at the dining room table, surrounded by reams of lists. Maybe it'll work, her idea of cooking for visitors, combined with cookery lessons online, blogging, as young Shaggy calls it. He also reports nothing but good things about the website thus far.

I, therefore, leave for the library with a hopeful heart. And luxuriate in the thought that after today, I'll be off for two days in a row, a rare occurrence. Life is sure looking up.

Tomorrow, we go back to police headquarters and let the hypnotist do their thing. Then we sit back and let the police interview DeSant, if Mr. White Cuffs is indeed him. And then, bang! The cops will be that much closer to "catching a thief," in Betty's cinematic phrase.

No heavy lifting on our part. Effective but subtle, worthy of the great Monsieur Poirot, if I may say so myself.

***

On my return, a few hours later, the dining table is still covered in papers. But everything is now arrayed in neat piles. The sitting room is equally tidy, with a bunch of candles arranged over the surfaces, already lit, in advance of the night. Through the arch leading from the sitting room, where I've deposited my briefcase, I see that Mo is busy in the kitchen.

"Remember, Betty is coming for nibbles!"

"As if I'd forget. A great start to the weekend. I can't wait to tell her I've been vindicated."

"Oh, Ollie, you make it sound like what's-his-name was after you, ready to throw you in prison again."

"The fearsome Javert, yes. Best musical ever!" I shoot back, humming a few bars. I then switch to a more serious tone as I get ready to mount the stairs. "Those who have not endured the iniquity of justice have no idea what it is to suffer its effects."

I must say, after this incident, I have a renewed sympathy for what it must be to have the police look at you as a criminal simply because of your gender, your sexual orientation, or your race. Because you were simply in the wrong place at the wrong time.

"Too bad we won't get to meet Manny," yells Mo, after one of her usuals, "Oh, you."

"I really want to meet the famous Manny Manuel, the Brats Boss of Chicago. I'd like to discuss some tax stuff with him."

From a distance, she can't see my eyebrow quirk up, my standard "Mo, please explain," commonly deployed after one of her wacky pronouncements. My sister lapses into silence, however. Curiosity prods me to move in the direction of the kitchen. With Mo, you never know. I see her then carefully adding some greenery to a dish on the counter.

"And what do you suppose he has to say about our taxes? Given that he's a billionaire and we're on Social Security?"

"Laugh if you will, but I think I'll ask about money havens. Legal ones, of course. The taxes on Social Security are a scandal. A disgrace, I tell you."

"I'm pretty sure there are no tax havens for little guppies like us. But you're not getting any pushback from me on the topic of taxes, trust me. The very word makes me ill. So, what are we having?" I finish, in a happier tone, joining Mo by the kitchen counter.

"Well, today's meeting with Detective Citroën inspired me. Voila! Guacamole, homemade chip, nachos, assorted boh-ta-nas," Mo answers with a newfound expertise with the Spanish language that surprises me. As I said, with Mo, you never know. "And to drink Margaritas. With supermarket tequila, before you go and start grumbling."

"Deep sigh, Mo," I answer, letting the Citroën go in my exasperation. "You do remember she told us she's Puerto Rican, right? Puerto Rican, as in *not Mexican*?" I air quote. "What happened to your vast knowledge of Latino cuisines?"

"Laugh it up, but I did date a Peruvian ophthalmologist before... Well, before you know who. Ramon would come over to keep me company after Gian died. Once, he even showed me how to make ceviche."

"Is that what they call it in old Peru? Making ceviche?" I move my eyebrows up and down, a la Groucho, and at the same time, I help myself to a cucumber thingy. "Yikes, that's hot!"

"Ollie Howard, you have a mind like a sewer," Mo fires back as she slaps my hand. "Unfortunately, with the price of sushi-grade fish these days, the ceviche was out," she adds with a meaningful look in my direction. There's that look again! Joan-of-Arc-on-her-way-to-the-bonfire.

"These are the only Latinx dishes left on my repertoire," she finishes, adding a bowl of cilantro to the tray.

"Right on, sister. But I'm pretty sure it's not pronounced Latin-knee-ex."

"Oh, you," Mo sighs, just as Bert begins to announce a visitor.

BETTY

The cottage is perfect. I can hear a barking dog coming from the inside, but I stand perfectly still at the foot of the staircase, my back to the door, drinking in the greenery around me in huge gulps. Like a painter at an art museum, a view of a lush garden brings out the creative soul in me.

A huge banyan tree spreads its lacy branches over the front of the property. Beneath it, assorted birds of paradise, fire bushes, and wooly cycads nestle between banana shrubs; the whole of it is surrounded by mounds of cannas, arrowheads, and well-named monsteras. In the warm air lingers the perfume of a crepe jasmine, its flowers competing in showiness with Chinese fringe flowers plants and trusty oleanders.

Heavenly, this spot is heaven, as far as I'm concerned, even if the house itself may have seen better days. An old-timey Florida cottage fronted by a deep porch, its once yellow walls now muted to a deep cream. If only I had time to explore the plantings a bit more. The barking, however, has become loud enough to alarm the whole neighborhood.

I finally mount the stairs, promising myself a visit to the spot, right between the garage and the fence separating the cottage from the mansion next door, where I noticed a collection of rare curcumas in bloom.

"Down, down! It's our friend, Betty, you silly, silly dog," Ollie booms as she holds the door wide open for me, a few moments later, struggling to hold a dog back. No doubt I'm about to meet the famous Bert.

After a sniff in the direction of my shoes, however, it turns around and marches right back into the cottage. I feel strangely dismissed.

It takes me a few seconds to get used to the dim interior. Straight ahead, I see a wide, dark-floored hallway leading to a staircase, bisecting the cottage in two. To the right, there is a room completely lined with bookcases—no surprise there—a dozen or more votive candles sizes arrayed along the shelves. A delicious mix of patchouli and something else I can't recognize hovers in the air. The well-used furniture is covered in navy canvas, piped in white.

Our destination is to the left, where an arched dining alcove leads to what can only be called, generously, a vintage kitchen. I haven't seen Formica like that since I was little when I'd count out the little beige half-moons for Ma. From behind a counter, I can see Maureen waving me welcome.

After a few hugs of greeting and even more barking, Ollie and I follow Maureen outside, our hands filled with platters and bowls. Circling as if trying to catch its own tail, Bert accompanies us through the wide French doors. Before me is a small, paved esplanade and an unexpected vista.

A small lake, complete with a teeny, tiny island—the kind that would hold two castaways in a cartoon—abuts the rear of the property. Another riot of flowering bushes, nestled under areca palms, circles the old-fashioned wrought iron dining set on the patio.

Today, the table is set for three with embroidered linen placemats with matching napkins next to what appears to be real bone porcelain plates, and can it be? Waterford glassware.

Around the lake sits a fair number of houses, some very extravagant from the silhouettes I can discern in the waning light. Amazing what builders can fit into a standard old Naples lot. A couple of dogs jump around crazily across the way. Where have I seen those brown and white shapes before? They continue to bark for a few more seconds and finally retreat inside.

Bert, however, insists on standing close to the edge of the water, still barking, as we take our seats at the table.

"Here we are, dear. So happy you could join us. Bert, give it up, will you? You showed those two up," Ollie cries out, patting her side. Bert ignores her summons and continues to advance perilously close to the pond with a menacing growl.

"Oh, Maurice and Chevalier are two cuties. They're pedigreed corgis, like Elizabeth's," Maureen answers, lighting the three hurricane lamps lined in the center of the table after giving me another hug in passing.

"But Bert is the better watchdog," comes Ollie's quick reply as I nod sagely to Maureen. Elizabeth, what Elizabeth? Oh, that Elizabeth. I simply nod again, as I realize Ollie is staring at me, as if awaiting my response. Another nod of my head and she continues, happily.

"Those Irish wolfhound ancestors of his really show up. Not for anything, the Romans exalted the Irish *canes* for their fierceness in fighting wolves," she adds, sounding like the history professor she resembles. This evening, her short hair is even spikier than usual, and she's wearing a black, square pair of glasses.

"Oh, is that what he is?" I ask finally, trying to suppress a grin. I'm no expert, of course, but if there's any Irish wolfhound in Bert — now settling with much snuffling at our feet — that ancestry is long lost to the ages.

"Darling, I don't think you should keep calling him a wolfhound," Maureen interjects, finally done unwrapping dishes and trays. "Remember what they told us at the refuge. Pure American m-u-t-t," she finishes, mouthing exaggeratedly in my direction.

I already know the sisters well enough to see where the conversation is heading. Before it can degenerate into one of their exchanges, I intervene. "Lovely place you have here, ladies."

As I look at the two beaming faces before me, I am ashamed to remember I doubted their honesty, even for a few seconds. How easy it is, I realize, to doubt people when the circumstances seem dead set against them.

"Oh, this place is all Mo's. It's been in her husband's family ever since the first Brian bought it. Back at the beginning of the last century. Brian 'Boru' O'Bryan," Ollie adds. "The first of the family to arrive from the old sod. And a fine example of a Chicago bootlegger, if I ever heard of one."

"Ollie, what will Betty think? Ignore her, please. Old Mr. O'Bryan, God rest his soul, actually spent years laboring away to establish one of Chicago's most elegant eating establishments."

"Have it your way, Mo. I believe the property was even more impressive back in the good old Prohibition days," Ollie continues with a smug smile at her chagrined sister. "Boru O'Bryan, that saintly soul," she says, crossing herself gleefully, "had the foresight to buy the whole block, lake, and island included. Those parcels were sold during the Depression."

"At one point, the property included a real chickee hut,

woven by descendants of the local Seminole. It blew away during one storm. One of the last original cottages in Naples left standing, built with tabby…" The next second, Ollie closes her lips firmly.

Obviously, keen as she is to continue in the professorial vein, we've not seen each other for three days. There's much to catch up with. Ollie puts the rest of the lecture away with a deliberate shrug of her shoulders.

"We are back in the game, Betty dear. Mo, take it away," Ollie announces then, pouring three generous servings of frosty Margaritas, as Maureen begins to describe their visit to the police.

As I listen, interspersing a question here and there, I zero in on a dish of cucumber boats, totally covered in some sort of chili powder and filled with spicy peanuts, cilantro, and lime juice. Just one of a dozen dishes of what Maureen keeps insisting are "just nibbles." Thank heavens I didn't have dinner, is all I can think. Accompanied by draughts of the cooling Margarita, I soon feel myself almost levitating.

My walk home is going to be interesting, I decide, helping myself to some more of the cukes. "You mean you've gone from prime suspect to police witness?" I hiccup at the end of the sisters' combined tale.

For all their bickering, I have to say they make very effective narrators. Almost like an old married couple, one picks up where the other leaves off.

"That's exactly it. But I must admit, Detective Cintron was very persuasive. Our civic duty and all that. A very professional young woman, I'll give her that—"

"—with a lovely head of curls," interrupts with a giggle Maureen, who, in the last hour, has sampled from the Margarita pitcher with gusto.

"Really, Mo? I was on my way to the women's prison in Ocala, and you had time to notice her hair?"

"And a nice, curvy figure," Maureen continues, happily ignoring Ollie's gaze of disbelief as she pushes a platter of petite fish tacos towards me. "So very sad, the way so many girls starve themselves these days. Too bad her wardrobe lacks pizzazz. She was back to wearing a white shirt tucked into black slacks. I wonder if Sak's would consider making a line for female detectives..." Maureen lets the sentence die unfinished, given that Ollie appears ready to do her physical harm.

"As I was saying...Cintron was very persuasive," Ollie recovers the thread of the conversation with a ladylike sniff. "The good news is that now there's a good chance the case will be solved. Not only is the session with the hypnotist scheduled for tomorrow—"

"Hip, hip, hooray!" comes from the end of the table.

"But also, given that I held back the bit about DeSant—"

"We forgot. We forgot to tell them—" Maureen interrupts again with a happy shrug.

"Lord, love a duck, you're annoying. Okay, we forgot," Ollie concedes, "I was so sure something awful was going to happen when the police called us in. I was totally not myself. So yes, I'll admit we forgot to let the police know there may be an actual witness."

"But now, the chances that the watch will be found, with our help, are looking better and better. Again, found with our help, I cannot emphasize enough. So even if the hypnosis proves a wash and we split the reward with you DeSant—"

"Lovely man, lovely resh...restaurant."

"I'm cutting you off," Ollie remarks, moving the Margarita pitcher out of her sister's reach. "As I was saying... even if we have to split the reward with DeSant, it'll be happy endings all around for this particular case."

"To happy endings, then."

"Happy endings, yesh!"

"Happy endings, agreed. But let's not toast too quickly," Ollie interjects as Maureen and I clink our glasses. "It's not over until it's really over. Remember Xavier?"

Trust Ollie, the faithful reader of mysteries, to remind us there is still one outstanding crime in our immediate sphere. Earlier, I had offered to pick the sisters up for tomorrow's ceremony. Together, I thought, we could offer each other moral support. Or they could support me. We've had time to get acclimated to the news, naturally, but who would look forward to such an occasion?

Ollie's reminder lowers the mood around the table a notch or two. It is somewhat of a relief, therefore, when Maureen pipes in. "I wonder, do you think Octavio would mind if I named the mousse recipe after Xavier? I wouldn't want to seem disrespectful, naturally. Just a gesture from someone who met him once at his best. What a lovely young man he was."

"Why are you naming recipes after people, Maureen? Are you writing a cookbook?" I ask in in the brief silence that follows as Ollie seems to ponder the question.

"I don't see why not," Ollie answers after a short pause, only to give an encouraging nod in her sister's direction. "Go on, Mo. Tell Betty your news. Tell her about your plan."

The air is again abuzz with chatter as Maureen, first, and then Ollie, go on to describe the food venture with increasing enthusiasm. Given the ingeniousness of the menu I just sampled, I'd say Maureen has come up with a great idea. Some of the details need tweaking, of course, and I agree that pricing could be tricky, but the more I hear, the better a chance my friend has of making a go of her new business, I think.

Which is why I finally say, "You know, Maureen, I think you're on to something. If you want another pair of eyes," I add, slightly apologetically, "perhaps I could take a look at your business plan?"

For an instant, I almost fear I've said the wrong thing. Do they think I'm trying to show them up by trotting out my past business experience? Two faces stare at me, eyes wide open. The next second, however, I'm bombarded by a torrent of words of gratitude mingled with questions. I end up raising both my hands up in mock surrender.

"Yes, of course, I won't mind. And before you go on thanking me, just so you know, I'm venturing outside my comfort zone. But I did get my start in accounting eons ago. You know what else?" I pause then, only to continue in a rush. "Maureen, you should also talk to Manny. See what he suggests.

"In fact, why don't the two of you come over Sunday?" I add, as Maureen gasps. "Manny will be back then. He's really looking forward to meeting the two of you."

"And so are we," Ollie responds formally. There are times when punk princess Ollie resembles nothing better than a grand nineteenth-century duchess. At least, an aristocrat of the kind found in the Regency romances I love to read on the sly. Maureen, meanwhile, seems too overcome to answer.

As Ollie works on Sunday afternoon, we agree they'll meet Manny over lunch. I accept Maureen's offer of a pound cake for our lunch—no fool, I—and we continue to talk for what seems hours.

As the evening begins to close, night insects zapping around us, it seems we've just begun to enjoy ourselves. And yet, time is running out. Important news remains unspoken. Bits of chatter that seemed important at the time but that, in my present Margarita-ed state, I can't recall.

"Don't worry about it, darling," Maureen offers, patting my hand as we turn to the two flans—coconut and pineapple—that cap the "just nibbles" before us. "Push it to the back of the stove. It'll come to you just as you're falling asleep, you'll see. That's what I do when I can't remember something."

And so, it goes. Tantalizing bits about the web page that is being designed by one of Ollie's library pals and suspected suitor of another of her colleagues. So much fun, speculating about the romantic life of young people, even if they are strangers.

The discovery of the actual term for the alpha treats, courtesy of Brad; a name which not one of us can pronounce correctly, much less in our present condition. Even more early O'Bryan family history during Prohibition—as related by Ollie and hotly contested by Maureen—which has me almost spewing the decaf over the remains of my dessert.

Made giddy by the atmosphere, I almost go on to speak of my own plans about the future. "But let's save *something* for Sunday," I catch myself in time. "Tonight's about you, Ollie, finally freed from police suspicions. *And* your business venture, Maureen." I offer as I raise my glass in one last toast, this time made with water.

"To a happy future for all of us. Don't forget, then, Sunday at noon. And now it's time for me to take myself off. Look at that, ten thirty already. We'll soon turn into pumpkins."

Over one last round of giggles, Ollie offers to give me a lift home, but I wave her offer away. It is a beautiful evening despite the earlier rain, and a full moon is out, bathing the world in a silvery glow. That wonderful feeling of time spent with good friends, eating good food, chatting our cares away, and toasting our friendship lightens my spirit and my way home.

CHAPTER SEVEN

MO

This time, we did remember to tell the police. At least, I did. "That may be Philippe DeSant, owner of the Á Toute Á L'Heure downtown."

Ollie had to repeat the name because Detective Alexander did not understand me at first. "Yes, the Á Toute Á L'Heure, almost at the end of Fifth."

She butchered the name, of course. "It means, 'see you later,' in French," I added, always happy to be of help. I *don't* think it was confusion over the difference in pronunciations, but all I can report is with that bit of information, the young man straightened up with a start. It was like watching one of those long, hinged rulers unfold itself.

He stared at us for a couple of seconds — two small ears sticking out, like parentheses bracketing cute features — and then he opened the door, still without uttering a word. And that was that. We didn't see him again.

Meanwhile, it turns out that the session with the hypnotist comes later. First, we both underwent a "non-hypnotic structured interview." Conducted separately with each of us, in different offices, to maintain the integrity of our testimony, we're informed. It was basically a reconstruction of the events in a different order and from a different perspective.

Yawn. I still haven't heard how it went with Ollie's, but mine was most definitely a waste of time. Still, I'm not willing to poopoo hypnotism to my heathen of a sibling. Boring or not, as we drove south on Goodlette-Frank, I let her know the meeting had gone as I had anticipated.

"Totally normal, nothing to it." I may have even snapped my fingers under her nose. Such a common gesture; must not make a habit of it.

Of course, I don't expect to regress to past lives under hypnosis! Ooh, that Ollie. Can I help it if I'm an old soul? Open to any experience that will expand my awareness? Of course, I am. Mine is a particularly sensitive spirit. In fact, lately, I've often felt surrounded by a presence hovering just outside the reach of my consciousness, so close that I can almost sense their aura.

"Oh, Bertie, baby, will you please watch it? We don't need another fall, do we? Mommy's face is almost back to normal. Ollie, are you almost ready?" I yell up the stairs. It's a rare day when I'm done before my sister. "You know Betty's punctual to a fault!"

It may be that the memory of the next appointment— we're set for Monday with the hypnotist—keeps the Naples police in my thoughts, but the next second, I reach for my phone.

I need to speak to that nice Detective Citroën. Of course, a handwritten thank you would be more proper, but I don't have her address. There it is, I did remember to list her number in my contacts list. Carmen Citroën. Not only did she get me her mom's recipe overnight, but the detective also made sure to leave a printed copy with her partner, young Alexander, at police headquarters. How nice is that?

"Detective Citroën, it's Maureen Novak. How are you? Good. Listen, I know it's your day off, so I won't take too much of your time. Gracias, muchas gracias," I practiced in preparation. "I so appreciate you getting me that copy of the arroz con gandules," I take care to pronounce the name of the rice and pigeon peas dish carefully.

Nice child that she is, she is nothing if not dismissive, so I find myself taking the conversation in a direction I hadn't planned. "Here's the thing, detective. Oh, call you See-see? C-i-c-i, See-see, got it. Well, thank you very much. Then I insist you call me Maureen, then. Mrs. Novak is sooo ageing.

"Where was I going with this? Oh, yes! Here's the thing. The first taping of my blog is scheduled for Monday morning. Don't you love how techy that sounds? The first taping. That afternoon, we have the hypnotist. Yes, the interview went well, thanks for asking.

"I'm calling the first blog A Caribbean Culinary Adventure. A Caribbean Culinary Adventure," I repeat it to make sure I convey the importance of the occasion. "And as the main dish, it'll feature your mom's recipe.

"I found canned pigeon peas at Publix. Thanks for the suggestion. Would you consider joining us? Share some memories of your mom's kitchen and of growing up Puerto Rican in Jersey City? I'm all about cultural appreciation, not cultural appropriation."

When Cici doesn't turn me down right away, I venture right in. "I can't pay. Not yet, anyway. Oh, no payments allowed. That's great…. I mean, of course, of course. But surely, there's nothing in police regulations about doing a favor for a friend, surely?

"I'll repay the favor with food. You can tell me if I have your mom's recipe right. Even better, I could introduce you to some people close to your own age. Some young people from the library will be on hand Monday when Ollie takes over the shooting. Tomorrow's just a trial run.

"I thought…well, I remember you *did* say you're new

in town. And all of us," I finish, suddenly shy. "All of us, no matter our age, need friends at every new stage of our lives."

Not ten minutes later, with the detective's agreement in hand — I'm going to have to get used to calling her by her nickname, See-see — I find myself at the foot of the stairs again. "Betty's here!" I yell, just as my sister comes clattering down the steps.

Given the amount of time it took Ollie to get ready, I'm surprised to find her wearing one of her usual white linen get-ups. Ironed trousers, in honor of the formal occasion, I suppose, and redolent as always of Jean Naté cologne. A classic combination. I'm the first one to admit it. But I do wish that one of these days, my sister would give up those Chuck Taylor sneakers she wears every day, everywhere. Another classic, but oh-so-dingy classic, in this case.

For my part, I'm wearing my Issey Miyake chocolate brown shift, long-sleeved, with pleated accents in the back and a bateau neckline. So divine and so very itchy and hot. I know I'm going to be roasting alive. It came out in the fall-winter 1997 collection — such happy memories, buying it with Brian on an October trip to Manhattan — but given that the air conditioning in Betty's car no-doubt works, and the restaurant is also nicely cooled, I decided to honor the divine Octavio and his lovely Xavier by wearing one of my vintage best.

When Betty arrives at the door, she appears in her usual tones of ecru, cream, and brown, which suit her so well. It seems that a detour into tropical prints is wisely behind her. Today, she has paired her outfit with, yes, another pair of Ferragamo flats.

"Why didn't you just text? You didn't have to come get us!" I say as we go down the stairs, me hanging on to the rickety banister. I stare at Betty's choice of footwear with envy. My Valentino T-Strap Pumps are to-die-for fabulous, anyone would agree, but the three-inch heels are beginning to make themselves felt. *Heeeello, knees!*

"I forgot my phone at home. I didn't want to be late, so I didn't go back. I'm going to have it tied around my neck one of these days."

"Tell me about it. I long for the day we can all have microchips implanted in our brains," I hear Ollie say behind us, in perfect seriousness. "Just think it, blink, and there it is. 'Calling Betty,' in that chirpy voice of the phone assistants."

I turn and notice — with dismay that equals that of my protesting knees — that Ollie is reaching for that distressing "White Sox 2005 World Champs" cap of hers, which she always parks by the small table in the front porch, but she apparently thinks better of it. Thank heavens for small favors.

***

Betty, bless her splendid heart, believes in making use of the valet parking, and the restaurant is freezing. Never too cold for me, though! I know I wouldn't have lasted five minutes out on Fifth Avenue.

A bank of angry clouds, poised over Tamiami, is moving swiftly and is about to overtake us. The strong wind already smells of rain but does little to relieve the humidity. A crowd of holiday visitors scampers around us, directing worried glances at the threatening skies.

There is a large amount of people already gathered inside Á Toute Á L'Heure. Over the heads of those waiting to pay their respects, I can see Octavio and Brad flanked by a young woman. I assume Xavier's wife — his widow, now.

I don't know why I'm surprised by the size of the gathering. I suppose my reaction comes from my refusal to really dwell on Xavier's death these past few days. The fact has hovered in my consciousness, of course, but deep inside me, I cannot contemplate the thought of a young person dying before their time.

No, no, no. Not with my Dr. Molly in the ER. Not with Trey, out and about every day, on the L. I suddenly realize that avoiding thoughts of grisly occurrences is nothing new with me.

"Ollie, can you save my spot in line?" I ask, a few seconds into the wait. I can deal with introspection, or I can deal with high heels, but not both soul-searching and creaky joints at the same time. "I'm going to sit over there. My feet are killing me."

"Serves you right. Yeah, go ahead, you two. I'll signal when we're almost there."

I dismiss Ollie's grumpiness with a sniff—she's probably still sulking over my comment about her choice of headgear—as Betty and I move towards one of the few empty tables in the place. As we approach the back of the restaurant, dimmer than the rest of the already-dim space, I espy a familiar sight.

An enormous, framed poster of a magnificent clock almost covers the entirety of a niche in the wall. The vista is one of several prints displayed on the walls of the restaurant, I notice just then.

I am immediately swept to another, happier time. Gian and I strolling around the Île de la Cité, pausing beneath the Tour de l'Horloge, the Seine River running serenely at our backs.

"'To protect justice and defend the law,'" I quote from memory.

"What's that?" Betty is naturally a bit taken aback.

"My Gian, honeymoon number two, was a pro at Latin. All those years spent with the Jesuits. I only remember that bit, though, about protecting justice and the law. That's the Clock Tower, the oldest clock in Paris," I turn to Betty with a bit more enthusiasm, trying to disguise the sudden sadness brought on by the memory of poor Gian, gone so early.

"Gorgeous piece, all blue and gilt. It has ticked away time at the Conciergerie for centuries. Many of the French aristos were imprisoned there, at the Conciergerie, during the Revolution. Including Marie Antoinette."

"Dismal place, you have no idea how gruesome it is. Her son, the last Dauphin, was jailed there, too. They kept that little boy in a closet, literally a small windowless cupboard, until he went mad. Just thinking about that makes me sick. What an awful world we live in, Betty, where children die before their time."

BETTY

If I had expected Maureen's usual sunny disposition would lighten the unease I felt all day at the prospect of the memorial, that hope just crashed and burned. The conversation has taken a turn for the dark. Between the memories of her second husband and that awful place she's talking about, it is a grim afternoon at the restaurant on Fifth Avenue.

It doesn't help that the sunlight is practically gone by now. Huge sheets of water hit the windows of the restaurant the moment we walked into the place. Distant peals of thunder underscore the restrained chatter around us.

Mercifully, before long, Ollie gestures us to her side. A few seconds later, we come face to face with Xavier's family. First, I shake hands with Brad, somber and dignified. Then I whisper some words of condolence to Octavio, who doesn't seem to register my identity. I gently recall our previous meeting at the Cafe Tortoni, but his face remains locked in a gesture of uncomprehending grief.

If I thought the worst was over, however, the sight of the next person in line again dissuades me of any hopeful expectations. "Thanks for joining us today. I'm Anne Bianchi," says the young brunette next to Octavio, magnificently pregnant.

***

No sooner are we all done paying our respects to the family, by unspoken agreement, we retreat to a buffet table that has been set out opposite the receiving line. A few minutes before, if asked, I would have said I wouldn't be able to eat one bit of food for the rest of the day. And yet, here I am, piling my plate with dainty crab cakes, tapenade, cantaloupe slices, and crostini.

"Why is eating such a natural reaction to events like these, do you think?" I marvel as we make our way down the food line. My question remains unanswered. I espy an array of small cups of chocolate mousse at the end of the table, then. At that sight, I turn away with a jerky motion, almost spilling the food I've just served myself.

Maureen must agree the desert evokes sad reminders. As she finally joins me to a side, a cup of half-melted gelato rests on the side of her dish. "You should try it. It's pistachio, homemade. Ollie doesn't care for gelato. Go figure. Her favorite is plain chocolate from that ice cream place down Fifth, almost by Tamiami. Do you know it?"

"Well, that was delicious," she adds after my silent nod of assent. "I don't know about you, though. I don't think I can ever bring myself to come back here for a very long time. Too many horrid associations."

She then looks around and asks almost apologetically. "Will you go with me to get DeSant's permission to use the soufflé recipe? It's going to be a while before they move to the actual memorial," she nudges me with a gentle elbow.

If anything, the line is longer than it was when we first arrived. The wait staff continues to travel between the kitchen and the dining room, laden with trays.

"Ollie's library colleagues are coming tomorrow morning to show us how to set up. Early, they know we have a lunch date. Then, they will return on Monday to supervise Ollie for the actual thing. She'll be my camerawoman; take over from...Shaggy. Ollie, dear heart, what's his real name?" Maureen adds, turning to the end of the table. "I can't possibly keep calling him Shaggy."

It is then that we notice that Ollie has left our side and slipped away unnoticed while Maureen and I were eating.

***

We both spot her at the same moment. She is off in a corner, talking to a statuesque woman dressed in a flamboyant purple and black caftan, a mess of grey hair streaked in pink piled high on top of her head.

"That's Harriet Stratemeyer. Have you heard of her? She's one of our local celebrities. Ollie must know her from the library. Helen's often there, holding readings and signing books for fans. Her mysteries sell in the millions, I'm told," Maureen confides in my ear.

I stare at the unknown woman for a few seconds more. In another age, I decide, she would've been described as an "authoress of renown." A fearsome female. Better yet, one of the real Amazons of antiquity. If postures were t-shirts, Stratemeyer' would read, "Gladly suffering no fools, since forever."

I wonder what she and the equally plain-spoken Ollie have to say to each other. I turn, the beginning of a comment on my lips, to see Maureen's expectant look. "Oh, yes, the recipe," I apologize as I prepare to follow her.

It takes a few minutes of asking from the passing wait staff, but we finally find DeSant is in his office. To his credit, he has kept to the margins of the celebration. Given his personality — or at least what was in evidence on the night we met him — I would have expected him to be front and center. Or at least, sharing the receiving line with the Bianchi family.

The light in his office is on. After a short knock, I follow

Maureen in, hardly waiting for the "come in!" that is pro forma in business settings. DeSant is sitting behind a large desk, his head low. It seems obvious the day is taking a toll on him, too. The next instant, he looks up, finds us standing by the door, and slams a drawer with a definite thud.

"Hello, there. You probably don't remember me. My name is Maureen Novak. We visited your restaurant three or four nights ago. We met you and Xavi then," she finishes plainly.

"Of course, I remember you. How are you, ladies, today?" DeSant answers. I can't tell whether he remembers us, in fact, but he's certainly an experienced restaurant owner, for whom making strangers feel as if they're old friends is all in a day's work. For her part, Maureen is composed, with no sign of her previous flirtatiousness as she goes on.

"You had your dessert chef, Felipe, show me how to make your chocolate mousse."

"That's right, I did. Now, I remember. What can I do for you, ladies?"

"Could I use the mousse recipe for a new business venture I have in mind? I'd give you full credit, of course. I'd even recommend the Á Toute Á L'Heure in my blog. We won't be competing for your customers, I can assure you. You see, my plan is to—"

At that moment, the landline on DeSant's desk rings loudly. "Hang on," he says, holding his finger up. "Yeah, babe? Can't make it? No worries. I'll call a ride then. They said I can pick the car up whenever. They're open late.

"Dealer tried to apologize," he adds, throwing himself back easily into the chair, the long cord dangling by his side. "Said it was a bitch locating parts for the gearbox. I'm gonna change places, I'm telling you. Three days wait, no loaner, no courtesy pick-up? Forget that! It's okay, don't worry, babe. See you later."

He hangs up and stares at us with an impatient "you still here?" look on his face, he's obviously too polite to voice.

"As I was saying, the recipe for the chocolate mousse," Maureen begins her explanation again, only to have DeSant cut her off.

"Whatever you're planning, I'm sure it's all good. Yeah, sure, go ahead. Use the recipe. In fact, while you're still here, ask Felipe where he sources his stuff. I know he usually gets us good deals," he finishes, accompanying us to the door.

Maureen and I trade the first true smiles of the afternoon as we exit back into the restaurant. She seems a little stunned by the ease of obtaining the permission. No explanation, no description, just like that, she got it.

"How soon are you making the mousse?"

"Soon. I didn't finish telling you all the news."

"Tomorrow's trial, you mean?"

"'Yes. But wait, there's more,'" Maureen giggles as she quotes the old commercial. "I also have a recipe from Detective Citroën. A Puerto Rican recipe. So, the first blog will have a Caribbean theme. Avocadoes grow in the Caribbean, right? So now, I'll add the mousse to the menu. I even came up with a name for it. *Xavier's Gift of Chocolate*. Nice, right?" she adds when she sees my nod of agreement.

"Oh, fabulous, there's Felipe," Maureen gushes, pointing towards the kitchen entrance doors, where the chef, still sporting his pirate-style bandanna, is holding court, surrounded by a group of young people.

Ollie is nowhere to be found, Maureen grabs my hand, and we rush towards the group. Just a few paces from the chef, however, the door to the ladies' bathroom opens. Out steps Anne Bianchi, her black dress tented prominently before her.

"Every fifteen minutes, without fail," she says with a grimace, pointing to the door marked "Mesdames."

"Lord, yes. I'd forgotten," I agree, with great sympathy.

"By the time we're done, we'd probably spent a year on the toilet, easy. How far along are you? Aren't you almost due?"

"A couple of weeks. And then I'll be meeting her." At that stark reminder of her loss, we offer our condolences again.

"Thanks, ladies. It means a lot to me that you met Xavi only once and are here today. And yes, what a sad, crazy day this is turning out to be. Right as Uncle Tavio and I arrived—Brad was still parking—we heard the Naples police were here to see the boss. He was in there for a while with them, in his office."

We make suitable noises of agreement. How do you say, "We hope they catch your husband's killer soon," in a social setting? We wait instead for her to make the first move toward the receiving line.

"Xavi and I met right around here, in fact," she continues, apparently not ready yet to rejoin them. A smile softens her face. Round cheeks, generous rosy lips, and wide brown eyes give her the air of a Renaissance Madonna. Her hands, small and childlike, do not seem capable of bearing the burden that lies ahead for her and her baby.

"Not the most romantic spot in the world. I had just started waiting tables that day. And as my opening act, I tip a glass of red wine over a client's white skirt. I'm dying. For sure I'm getting fired, I think. But Xavi rushes over, a wide smile, a can of soda water, and plenty of napkins in hand."

"By the time he's done, the lady is apologizing *to me* for jolting my hand. That's my guy. He's like that with everybody. Everybody loved Xavi. He brought out the best in everybody. In fact, Philippe threw us a small wedding breakfast here. That's how much he liked him."

"He's another one, the boss. Always ready to give in to generosity. And now, here we are, all of us. Saying goodbye to Xavi."

I, for one, am ready to bring the conversation to a close, before it becomes too painful for our new acquaintance. But Anne goes on to show a steel-like spirit underneath that soft Madonna-like exterior.

"I know Xavi's gone, but he'll always be with me," she says, patting her stomach. "My worry is Uncle Tavio. I don't know how he'll manage to go on. True, he'll have her with him, night and day, but even so, it's going to be awful.

"Xavi and I moved in with Uncle Tavio and Brad a month ago," she explains to a chorus of tsk-tsks from Maureen and me. "In fact, it was their idea. They gave us the use of their in-laws' cottage for free. Fancy us in Port Royal!"

"Move in for a while and save money for a house, they said. We'd been looking at townhouses in Golden Gate. In the meantime, I was supposed to help at the Tortoni while I'm nursing. And we were all going to take turns looking after the baby. Even Brad. Can you imagine? He'll have her in cashmere onesies in a day," she chuckles gently.

"The move was also meant to give me time to plan for after she's weaned. I'd been thinking of quitting the restaurant business, but who knows now. Who the heck knows what's going to happen now," she repeats, shaking her head. "Life stopped making sense a week ago. I even heard that some of our friends have been let go. I think the publicity around the accident is turning people off, poor Philippe."

"Totally irrational, I agree," Maureen chimes in as Anne finally seems to be running out of conversation. "But I was just telling Betty. It will be difficult for regulars to return for a while."

As I see Anne begin to move away, I jump in. "Don't let me leave without your phone number. You'll have to write it down for me. I forgot my cell at home. When you're ready, give me a call. I'm sure, make that, *I'm positive* I can help you find a new job when the time is right."

With that, Anne nods, a forlorn smile on her fresh face, and moves away.

***

Thankfully, the occasion did not end as dismally as it began. A short period after the buffet table was cleared, two young men moved towards the center of the restaurant and claimed everybody's attention with the traditional clinking of spoons on glass flutes.

Meanwhile, the wait staff circulated, handing all those in attendance a glass of champagne. At the end, the waiters, too, grabbed a drink and joined the group. Philippe DeSant, now occupying a corner, kept a respectful distance from the family.

"Let it be known, good people, far and wide, that today we gather to celebrate the life and times of our friend, Xavier Bianchi," begins one of them, a strapping, handsome blonde who resembles the star of any superhero movie. Only missing is the hammer and the cape. As the crowd raises their glasses, he goes on. "Let's first remember our friend's attachment to his classic Mustang —"

"Always in the shop!" yells a voice from the crowd, with a whoop of laughter. "Let's honor his passion for football," continues the second speaker, a young Hispanic man with a bun high on his head, like half of the young men around Felipe.

At those words, a chant of "la-doh-seh, la-doh-seh, la-doh-seh " erupts from the group in the back of the room. At least, I think that's the cry, my restaurant Spanish is a bit rusty.

"Cheevas, not Boca!" Felipe, the dessert chef, intones with a grin from the back, shaking his head, only to be booed down.

"Doh-se means twelve," whispers Maureen, displaying a sudden mastery of Spanish I would never guess was hers.

Ollie — back with us — is apparently a newcomer to her sister's linguistic skills, too.

"And what, pray tell, is the twelve? Who are these twelve? Twelve lords a-leaping?"

"No clue, darling."

"Quiet down, back there," says the athletic blonde, trying to calm the exuberant group around Felipe, who keeps chanting in Spanish. "We know, we know, soccer is all."

"Soccer? What soccer? Football, gringo!" is the good-natured answer to his attempt. "Viva el Boca Junior!"

"As I was saying before I was so rudely interrupted — I heard that *gringo*, Garcia, don't think I didn't — let's celebrate Xavi's many passions. His passion for life. His joy. His exuberance."

"Let's pay tribute to his character," his companion continues then. "His attitude towards all people, of all races, all ages, all walks of life."

Ollie decides to join the celebration then, hollering, "Hear, hear!" and slapping one hand on a nearby table.

"And, of course, I saved the best for last," the young Hispanic man adds, a gentle smile on his face. "Let's remember and honor his love of family. The lovely Anne. Where are you, Annie? Don Octavio, don Brad? Front and center, por favor. Let's all raise our glasses and let's drink a toast to our compañero, Xavier Bianchi. To Xavi and all those he loved. Long may they prosper and keep his memory alive! Cheers!"

Champagne flutes are raised all around. With the toast, Anne and Octavio fuse in an embrace, Brad standing right behind them as if guarding their backs. I turn away then, too moved to pay attention to what happens next. I do notice my tears are duplicated on the cheeks of some of the faces around me.

The mood in the restaurant has shifted. While some of the older people in attendance begin to slip out — no doubt emotionally exhausted, I know I am—a crowd of youngsters surrounds Xavier's family. It appears the testimonial unlocked a flood of happy memories in Xavier's colleagues and friends, a treasure trove they are happy to share with Brad, Octavio, and Anne.

I approach them, meaning to get Anne's phone number. Xavier may be beyond all earthly help, but I know I can help his wife and daughter. As I get closer, however, I realize now is not a good time. Anne is holding hands with Octavio and Brad, each on each side of her. Wide smiles, mingled with tears, are also on display on their faces.

I hear Octavio's voice, gently agreeing with a heavily tattooed woman who's holding his hands in both of hers. "Sí, sí, that was mi hijo." I don't need a translator to recognize a father's expression of deep pride in his son. In that, we are all the same.

OLLIE

Must admit, maybe I was mistaken about the creep. DeSant did not seem quite as slimy today as he did previously. He did behave with utmost discretion. Plus, there was that gesture at the conclusion of the memorial, when he moved to the center of the room, right by the two young speakers, and claimed everybody's attention.

"Well said, gentlemen. Just a quick announcement on my part. We all need to recuperate after the loss we've experienced at the Á Toute Á L'Heure family. To all the staff, tomorrow's on me. I'll see you all back here on Tuesday, bright and early. Let's have a Fourth to remember!"

With the unexpected gift of a paid Sunday off, the mood at the Tutti Frutti is close to jubilant as we abandon the place. Even Octavio seems happy, nodding in agreement, obviously touched by DeSant's words about the Tutti Frutti "family." Much as it pains me, I'll grant that was a thoughtful action on his part.

As for us, other than Betty mentioning something about Anne Bianchi's phone number, which she failed to get, we ride back in a silence that signals our collectively drained spirits. If only we could share the mental bounciness of the young.

"For there is assuredly nothing dearer to a man than wisdom, and though age takes away all else, it undoubtedly brings us that." I got news for you, Cicero, my good man. There's many an occasion when I would gladly swap some of my sagacity for a tad of the emotional resilience of youth.

***

Even Mo is unusually quiet as we arrive at the cottage. With Betty refusing an invite to come in, pleading a headache, it is a quiet evening for us.

And if Xavier's memorial wasn't enough of a letdown, later, I discover my sister on the edge of her bed, weeping softly over Gian into one of her ridiculously small lacy hankies. Which she is apt to do, usually around their wedding anniversary or the date of his death. But why the tears today, she won't say.

I hold Mo's palm, letting my hand occasionally stray to her back to pat it rhythmically as I sit silently next to her. The evening sun paints golden bars on the wooden floor at my feet. Mo's room overlooks the side of the cottage and is usually flooded with soft, green light filtered through the two windows.

I prefer to keep a watch on the neighborhood. Which is why I occupy the room over the porch, although that choice forces me to gaze at the monstrosity across the way: the misbegotten love child of a Tuscan palazzo and the Petit Trianon. Ugh! Every night, as I draw the shade on my one window, I silently bid its garish façade goodbye and good riddance.

The remaining bedroom upstairs is still known as "the trunk room." Tiny, but in use when Mo's grandbabies are in residence. I sometimes imagine I can hear the giggling from the many "dolls" — silk stockings gartered under the knees — that no doubt accompanied "that saintly Mr. O'Bryan" on his Florida sojourns and who stored their luggage there.

Mo and I sit, for a good long while, on the edge of her bed. My sister's tears are soon spaced farther apart as I continue to stroke her back in small circles. A steady hand is the only balm, other than my presence, that I can offer her. What is there to do when our loved ones suffer the re-opening of old wounds? Keep a silent watch by their side, make gentle noises of reassurance, stroke a beloved face, that is all.

As I continue to keep Mo company, my thoughts soon drift to tomorrow's agenda. All is ready for work, coffee set, clothes laid out. First item of the day, of course, will be a quick trial run of the filming. Then lunch at Betty's — immensely grateful she didn't suggest anything earlier — and the meeting of Manny, he of the frequent and mysterious trips.

We'll zip back home, then I'll hop on Coral, and next, it's off to the library for me. I'm so close to locating a manuscript on Naples' early history that it is as if I can almost smell the peppery scent of the moldy paper. A better day is on the horizon, indeed.

***

Eventually, Mo's tears stop for good, and we move downstairs. No dinner for us, naturally, so I settle on my comfy old seat by the bookcase. The contentment that usually flows through me when I grab one of my well-loved mystery novels, however, eludes me.

For one, there was that notion that popped up like a clown-in-a-box — good lord, those things are sinister — as I got ready for the ceremony earlier today. I suspect the idea was the brainchild of my interview with the hypnotist-that-wasn't.

My sister's session may have been fine, but mine was a total bust. Another round of who-where-when-what that seemed to go nowhere. But it did plant a seed in my brain, I will say that much. Add to that the unexpected gift—I don't know if "gift" is the correct term, but it'll do—of running into Stratemeyer at the Tutti Frutti.

Helen is a know-it-all of incredible, nay, historical, proportions. I know, I know. Brainy women of a certain age get saddled with that term. But in this case, it is accurate. It takes one to know one, as the saying goes. Smarticles, in fact, is the name my brothers still call me on occasion, drat all four of them.

But the woman is willing to expound about her craft at length. Try shutting her down once she gets going, in fact. Were I Mo, I'd be prattling about the Universe sending me a message I dare not ignore. Why not give it a try, then? Cur non, indeed.

There, Betty's exploring a new venue. She hinted as much last night. Mo has her business plans. Why should I be the only one left behind? So, I put Christie to the side and reach for my laptop instead. After a period of laborious typing, I am ready for a cup of energizing chai.

"You've been very quiet. Are you sure you're okay now?" I can't help but note, as I place the kettle on the stove. Mo is in the dining room, presiding over her many bundles of lists, stickered folders, and decorated notebooks.

"Turns out all the recipes for Octavio's alpha treats I find are in Spanish, drat."

"Wait, you're Interneting? What's gotten into you, Maureen Mauverneen?"

"Betty Manuel is not the only person re-inventing herself. You did catch that bit about *saving it for Sunday*? I wonder what she's up to?"

While the water heats, Mo and I speculate about our friend's plans, but we leave that to the side. Tomorrow will come soon enough. So, I set the small, hand-painted teapot to the side, and I then fetch my laptop to help with the search.

"Why do you keep the volume so low?" I ask first, as a teeny, tiny Spanish voice continues to echo from her cellphone.

"Don't. Leave my cell alone," Mo answers, slapping my hand away. "Nothing wrong with my hearing. And I don't like a rude phone." As I often say, with Mo you never know. A rude phone, I ask you.

"How do you spell those things again?"

"A-l-f-a-j-o-r-e-s," Mo spells laboriously by my side.

"What happened to your recent mastery of Spanish? Nothing doing," I finally concede. "I can't find anything in English. Talk about elusive. The Scarlet Pimpernel's got nothing on them."

Lame joke done. I balance the teapot on top of the laptop and return to my perch. I retake the outlining, but eventually, all my ideas peter out. I move to a Dorothy Sayers then. Nothing as reassuring as an old friend in times of mental and spiritual unrest.

Like that freakishly tiny voice in Mo's cellphone, the events of the last few days, however, won't be silenced. The crowded pier. The stolen watch. That dratted first visit of the Naples detectives. Dinner at the Tutti Frutti. Young Xavier's death. That disappointing second visit to police headquarters. The banal round of where-were-you-when with the hypnotist technician.

Maybe it's the caffeine in the chai, but no matter how hard I try to concentrate on Lord Peter's escapades, I find myself returning to Roger Ackroyd.

"*Wondering if there was anything I had left undone.* Mo, does it ring any bells with you?" I finally yell. "'*Wondering if there was anything I had left undone...'"*

"Of course, it rings a bell! You keep insisting on reading it over and over. What is it, three times in as many days?"

My sister, it is widely known, is prone to exaggeration. But the import of the passage in Christie, continues to haunt me. Like a pointy broken tooth, a painful tongue can't resist prodding, over and over, the notion of "something's left undone" persists in my brain. Not mine, the negligence. No, siree, not me!

Somebody I have been close to recently; bore it markedly enough to have made an impression that continues to nag at me. *Something's been left undone.* But what, what was left undone? When, where?

INTERLUDE #4

Doxies! Jades! I should not have expected the hedge-born to recognize a knight of my quality. The Uncommonly Tall One, as I shall be calling her henceforth, is a deuced scold. And given to spouting arrant nonsense. *Queens of the Celts...* As if I would deign to serve in the armies of the mad Hibernians.

Her companion, the Midge, is a fizgig. I would almost deem her a natural, given her delight in childish prattle. Although I will grant her a faithful service to her Norman overlords, given her spouting of a bastardized form of that noble tongue. And yet, there is nothing to be done but entrust myself to the care of these two, for the nonce, despite the bleak prospects ahead.

There was blather earlier of yet another reduction of the rations. No small beer to break my fast; no muscadine to imbibe at supper; no pandemain; no, not even a trencher. Thus far, I've been asked to survive on oddly packed numbles, served on a round. What am I, a mangy cur?

As befitting a man of my stature, I have tried for

resignation, to no avail. My pleas to the Heavens remain unanswered. This is forsooth the work of some devilish sorcerer. How can it not be thus?

The way stands clear 'afore me. I will raise the hue and cry anon among the yokels. This matter will not stand.

CHAPTER EIGHT

MO

The trial run went off without a hitch. True, Ollie wandered around the kitchen for a good while, gulping cup after cup of coffee in a desperate attempt to get her bearings, but in no time at all, she had recovered her wits, despite the unearthly, for her earliness of the chosen hour.

Nine o'clock, I ask you, what kind of person cannot be ready to face the world by nine o'clock in the morning? Ollie, my smarty-pants sister, that's who.

Thankfully, we had the mechanical expertise of Ayesha and, yes, young Shaggy. He insists I call him Shaggy. "Trust me, Mo, everybody else does. Why not you, too?"

As, at the time, he was busily chomping away at the breakfast treats I provided, I took that as a real indication of his larger-than-life self. I find people are most reliably authentic when they eat. Name me a person who judges other people's joy in food and drink, and they will often turn out to be a miser in everyday life. And in bed, too.

Shaggy it is, then. I must say he was everything I expected from Ollie's description. Lanky, auburn hair hinting strongly of clementines orange — good thing he's a male, is all I have to say — and easygoing. A few minutes into their arrival, he stood by the kitchen counter, holding a slightly concave posture and inhaling more scones than I ever thought one person could do without getting sick.

For her part, Ayesha proved to be a delightful young lady; her enviable complexion the delicious caramel of an expertly flambéed crème brûlée. I totally understand Shaggy, I must confess. I totally lost my heart to her enormous hazel eyes, presiding over a Cupid bow of a mouth in a heart-shaped face.

In fact, even before we started, I could not help but step up to her. "All real?" I asked, pointing at the extravagant fans of black lashes that surround the child's stunning eyes.

A scandalized cry of "Mo!!! Really?" came from Ollie, which, par course, went ignored. I cannot claim to know the latest fashion among the youth of today, but I can spot a fellow fashionista when I see one.

"All real. A gift from my yumma," smiled Ayesha, giving them a quick tug. "You should see my mom's."

"My, my. No mascara, either. No bad hair days, ever?" I add then, pointing to the creamy rose silk scarf that frames her features.

"Not a one. Only bad hijab days." We slap palms, and the trial run continues to its spectacular end.

God bless them, they make a cute couple. Not that they are aware they are a couple yet, of course. But one only had to see the tenderness towards each other, as they asked for a piece of equipment. That almost embarrassed hesitancy when they both reached out for a cable and their hands touched. It may take Shaggy and Ayesha some time, but they'll get there.

To be young and falling in love again. Although I, for one, am done with Cupid forever.

Instead, I will concentrate on the success of my business venture. The Universe is aligning itself, as I always knew it would. If only...if only said Universe would send me a pair of steady feet as I move down the new path before me.

Good thing today I wore my navy blue-and-white striped, wide poncho-like top and my very forgiving Chico white jeans. Lord, I love their sizes! No sign of trembling knees under those babies, not when anchored by Stuart Weitzman platform espadrilles.

Still, at the end, as we discussed the actual filming, my legs shook to such a degree that I had to grab the kitchen counter to steady myself, just as if I were embarking on a tree pose after a late night. How will I manage when the adventure begins for real, remains to be seen. I wish I were a braver person; I really do.

***

All morning musings are gone in a puff, dispelled like the warm air that blows around me, as we finally show up at Betty's. A good twenty minutes late. Turns out we badly miscalculated the time it would require Ollie to set up on her own.

What will Betty make of our tardiness? I don't want to consider. She, who's always early everywhere.

And why couldn't we take the Granny either, still eludes me. What can we have saved, timewise? Five minutes? It may be faster, but with me carrying the pound cake, I feel like I'm juggling a baby. I was so distraught over our delay, however, I didn't even fight Ollie over the stupid helmet.

We park Coral a few feet away from a very large RV that occupies the space in front of the garage. The garden around us, hidden from the street by a Naples hedge — so thick, they resemble small vegetable rooms — is beautifully planted with a multitude of tropical shrubs.

The dusty green fronds of some familiar-looking palms provide pools of sun and shade for plantings of colorful bromeliads. I think those are bromeliads. Groves of clacking bamboo — those I recognize, for sure — also protect the inhabitants from curious eyes on both sides.

It all makes for a spectacular frame for the Manuel's house, a modernist series of cement cubes seemingly linked by open-air corridors. "Don't we have a few of those palms in the yard?" I ask as Ollie presses the doorbell again.

"Probably. Nature Gone Wild could be the name of our yard."

It feels as if we've been standing by the door for a good five minutes—Ollie even has time for a quick chat with Fred the Aloe, in his ceramic planter by the front—when it finally opens.

Today is the day for lanky males. Make that, if Shaggy is lanky, the specimen before me is the width of a bucatini noodle. With a deep feeling of envy, I notice the waist of his jeans is gathered by the belt in a paper bag effect, which I don't think was intended. The man is that thin. He's also sporting a red and black Dollywood t-shirt, with a perky butterfly where the W should be, that accessorizes nicely with the twang that drips, like honey, from his mouth.

"You must be Miss Ollie and Miss Maureen. I'm Freddy." We are expected to know *of* him, it seems, because he makes no further effort to identify himself.

With the greeting goes the handsomest smile I've seen in a very long time. It transforms skinny Freddy into gorgeous Frederick, to which a set of remarkably even, gleaming teeth adds a touch of newscaster glamour.

"Come in, come in, y'all. Don't just stand there. Betty went out, oh, a good hour ago. Said something about ice cream," he continues. Surprise at the news keeps Ollie and I rooted in the doorway.

"I was just about ready to go, seeing as you good folk were expected for dinner...lunch to y'all," he corrects himself with a wink. "But when noon rolled around, Manny just went out, looking for her. Asked me to wait for y'all."

"What about her phone? She's not answering?"

"She doesn't have it. Poor thing, she spent plumb half an hour looking for it, even had me call it. Must be on vibrate."

"Lateness is not Betty's style at all. If it's all the same to you, Mr. Freddy," says Ollie, unusually formal, even for her, "we're gonna go and give Manny a hand. It's probably just a flat tire, I bet."

I know my sister. That's a definite note of concern in her voice. I don't get it. Sounds like Betty and Manny could be joining us at any moment. I deposit the pound cake with Freddy, however, and I follow her back to the Vespa.

Now that my hands are clear, I think of transferring my phone from the waistband of my pants and realize the jeans lack pockets. Make that, given the most recent expansion of my mid-section, the jeans lack usable pockets, unless I want to impale myself painfully on one hip.

I may be starting a food business, but I *must* stop sampling every dish.

I grow increasingly frustrated as I wrestle with the pants' waistband, which the sweat has rendered impossible to open. It's like trying to peel an unripe banana. There! I finally tuck my phone beneath my forgiving navy-and-white blouson. I blame all this trouble on the rushed departure, naturally. Otherwise, I would've grabbed any one of my mini crossbodies. To think I actually left the house without my lipstick. I shudder at the thought.

Of course, it doesn't help that while I scramble to rearrange my clothing, I have Ollie whispering two inches from my ear. "Come on, Mo, come on!" Something of Ollie's urgency finally transfers itself to me. Despite the humid air, the hairs on my arms feel like there's an electric storm coming.

Ugh, that Ollie. I mount Coral without a peep of protest about the stupid helmet. Again. Twice in a day, I've held my fire back about that contraption. It must be a new record for me.

Not ten minutes later, I signal to Ollie to stop at one side of the intersection of Third Street and Fifth Avenue. "Now, if the ice cream shop is at that end —" I begin, pointing ahead.

"How do you know where she went?" Ollie jumps in.

"Because I told her about your weakness for their plain chocolate, of course."

"So, if the store is just a couple of blocks down, in that direction... What could possibly be taking Betty so long? Do you think she stopped at the Tutti Frutti to get Anne's number? She was adamant about it yesterday. They must be open for lunch already."

"Why would she? DeSant gave everybody the day off, remember?"

As we pass the restaurant, however, a car parked in front pulls Ollie's head with the force of a magnet. The Vespa slows down for a heartbeat. And then my sister, the safest of drivers, completes the most reckless of U-turns. Several cars honk crazily behind us, a curse or two floating in our wake.

A BMW, resplendent from a recent wash, occupies not one but two parking spots in front of the Á Toute Á L'Heure. Under the almost-noon sun, its chassis sparkles so brightly that it's almost impossible to stare at it for too long. As coppery as a new penny, the extravagant vehicle seems to demand attention from the passing crowd.

In fact, during the few seconds we stare at it, sweat pooling beneath my helmet— ugh, that Ollie—a fair number of males stop by. Next, they walk the length of the car, singly or in pairs, shake their heads, some even whistle, and then continue their progress down the sidewalk.

"Why would DeSant be in today? What did Xavi call it? The Mighty Lemon?" Ollie queries follow each other so quickly that it takes me a couple of seconds to regroup.

"The Mighty Orange," I finally offer in response.

"I remembered because, you know, Granny Smith, green; Mighty Orange, orange."

"Would you call that orange, Mo?"

"I most certainly would. A burnt sienna, with very strong orange undertones. Parked out here to show it off now that he's got it back. It must've been a real pain for him, physical pain, to be carless, even for a few days. Men and their toys. Why, I remember Brian —"

"Whoa, Nelly. Back up, back up. What do you mean, carless?"

"There was something wrong with something. A box of some sort. Gosh, was DeSant ticked off! Me, I've always found the BMW technicians —"

"Since your *technician* is an alley mechanic in Immokalee, I don't see what you know about BMW. So, DeSant was carless this week? You're sure about that?" Ollie asks again. A strange note of something I can't identify underlines her voice once again.

"He waited three days for car parts, yes-I-am-sure," I answer, with a show of dignity despite her dig. One of us must act like an adult, I always say.

"At least, that's what he told somebody he called babe when he got a call yesterday. Betty and I were in his office, getting permission to use the mousse recipe."

"Figures. He's the type to call all women 'babe.' Let that be a lesson to you, Mo. Let's go in. My Spidey senses..."

OLLIE

"...are on full alert." I underscore that last bit with a chuckle. I'm hoping that making fun of my growing uneasiness will result in less of an embarrassment when Mo and I interrupt DeSant paying bills. And it turns out that, yes, Betty came out from the ice cream store to find her Land Rover had a flat tire.

And with those thoughts come the memory of skid marks on a cement curb, a damaged tree, its bark a white wound, a mess of trampled shrubs.

Inside, the long buffet board is gone. The rest of the tables are tidy, chairs leaning against white tablecloths already set up for the next working day. Cooler, even dimmer than when we were last here, the darkness is only interrupted by a bright light at the end of a short hallway.

I don't need Mo's whisper in my ear to confirm the corridor leads to DeSant's office. A quick knock, and in we go. I yell a bold "Hello? Hello?" as I enter, feeling increasingly foolish.

There's the missing Betty. Seated, her arms held back by something, a white rag stuffed in her mouth. In real life, a situation like that sounds like the set-up for a cartoon caption contest. "All Bowser had to say was 'no vet.'" Some silly, inconsequential New Yorker game like that; we've all played them a million times.

Until you detect the panic in the eyes. Too, too late, I realize the alarm in Betty's eyes is on our behalf. The door crashes behind me, unnaturally loud in the quietness of the office. There stands Philippe DeSant right behind us.

"I told you Betty was all right." This comment from Mo, who obviously still hasn't caught on to what is happening. Quick as a panther — a grey panther — I dart for the doorknob. "Ah, ah, ah. No, you don't," DeSant cautions, grabbing my hand with a jerk.

So much for the self-defense classes I've attended faithfully ever since I moved to Naples. All sensible thoughts fly out of my head next as he grabs the arm and turns it behind my back. "I insist you stay a while. *Cuor non*. What's that?"

I will not give him the satisfaction of answering. But then I hear sweet, sweet Mo answer, as always, "Why not. The motto of the Marquis... Hey, what's going on?" she adds, finally realizing we walked into the proverbial hornets' nest. How dangerous is this one nest? I'm afraid we're about to find out.

"Let her go! This instant! What's wrong with you, mister? Stop hurting my sister!"

"Why not?" DeSant answers with a hideous giggle. "In that case, if you don't want me hurting, sissy, I suggest you keep your mouth shut. And cooperate like two good little girls.

"Fine," he adds as I struggle in protest. Insult to injury. "Like good little women. That way, I won't have to hurt her." He then twists my arm again as if to add an extra emphasis to his threat.

Ignoring my yelps — I cannot help myself — DeSant next kicks a silver freezer bag towards Betty's feet. The mouth of the bag opens, and the smell of chocolate rises incongruously in the air as a container of melted ice cream skitters on the floor. "I couldn't bear to see those leather seats get ruined. You're welcome. Your car is safely out of the way, too," he adds, pushing something else in her direction.

I now realize Betty's arms are tied with what appears to be a mess of telephone wires. "Aren't you saying hi to your pals?" he singsongs next. "Blink once for hi, twice for nice to see you, both."

He seems to tire of goading Betty almost as quickly as the words are out of his mouth. He then addresses Mo and I with a note of almost complaint in his voice.

"You wouldn't believe the fight your girlie over there put up. But you'll play nice now, right?" he insists, over my poor shoulder, swiveling his head towards Betty once again. "You wouldn't want your pal to suffer unnecessarily, would you?" With that, he adds some extra torque to my arm.

"Turns out our girl stopped by to ask me for Annie's phone. Just her luck. She walked in on me at the wrong time."

"And what's that? The time you devote to oiling your hair?" Not the greatest verbal jab, I'll agree, but it's the best I can do. My shoulder goes on high alert next with another twist of his hand.

"That's Ollie's bad shoulder, mister," yells Mo with great indignation. She's starting to acquire that Mama Bear look her kids tease her about. I wish, I sincerely wish, however, she'd shut up and not give him any ideas, as DeSant toggles at my arm repeatedly.

"This one, you mean?" he asks, almost playfully. "Poor old thing."

I feel the bones of my shoulder grinding. My right shoulder, the site of a rotor cuff injury, was followed by a bout of frozen shoulder that never resolved itself. That shoulder. I think I'm going to pass out.

I don't have the heart to glance at Mo as I hear a soft sound of distress escape her lips then. "Well then, if you don't want Ollie hurt, be smart. Sit down next to your friend right over there. See what a nice girl she is been?"

"She has a name, mister," apparently, "mister" is the only insult my sister can muster under duress. "She's not a *girl*," I hear Mo splutter dramatically then. I imagine her pointing indignantly at our friend. What a moment for my sister to trot out her feminist CV. "*She's* Betty. Betty Manuel!"

And we have a trifecta! It seems today is the day for Maureen to provide no end of useful information to a man who has us at his proverbial mercy. A younger, strong man, one with who-knows-what sort of intentions towards us. That knowledge pops up, unwelcomed, into my mind, increasingly made hazy with pain.

"Well, well, not *the* Mrs. Manuel? Why didn't you say so before?" I bet anything the monster's eyes are gleaming at the knowledge. "I wonder how much the Brats Boss would...

"You know what, never mind that. I'm not cut out

for a life of crime. A life on the lam, on the other hand... The Roadster and the—the other thing will have to do me. Too bad."

At that, Betty's eyes positively glower. They may be brown, but they now acquire the reddish depths of a volcano about to erupt, I swear. On the heels of that notion, the office lights begin to flicker. Or maybe it's just me, as I feel my grasp on reality begins to slip. DeSant has begun to move me forward, pushing me by my twisted arm.

A loud sob escapes me then, and tears begin to gush down my face. The next thing I hear is Mo letting out a litany of moans. My poor, sweet Mo. DeSant and I finally come to a stop in front of Betty.

"I told you already. It was an accident. Would you like for me to take it away?" he asks his tone of voice now as reasonable as if he were checking a dinner reservation. "You look like you could use a long, deep breath. But no more biting, agreed?"

And then, without waiting for a nod, DeSant removes what turns out to be a napkin from Betty's mouth.

BETTY

"You bastard." My voice is such a hoarse, raspy gasp, even I don't recognize it.

"There's gratitude for you. Where's the nice lady of an hour ago, uh? The kind lady who came in asking for Annie's phone number? *I'd like to help her get back on her feet. I'm sure she and the baby could use our help,*" he mimics in a horrid falsetto.

"Must be nice to be so rich, so able to change people's lives with a flicker of a finger. Talk about privilege. Wave a wand, problems solved. Just don't forget to kiss my ass on the way out, you peasants."

Beside him, I see Maureen lower her head and grasp

her hands in front of her waist as if in prayer. Her repeated groaning as she presses her midsection with her folded hands almost drowns out his words.

DeSant stares at Maureen for a few seconds, shrugs his shoulders, and turns back his raptor eyes towards me. At that moment, he has acquired the look of an eagle, a harpy eagle, about to swoop in on some prey.

"How can you bring yourself to begrudge Anne my help, any help, after what you did to her?" I finally spit out. My words are almost garbled, I'm so furious.

"It was an accident! How many times do I have to repeat it? I wasn't thinking right. I panicked. When the kid came back with the schedule, I thought he'd found it—"

"The kid. He. It," I interrupt, fury making me reckless. "I see you have problems with language. Say his name. You thought *Xavier* found the *stolen watch* in your desk," I emphasize the words with such force I feel spittle flying out.

"Just as I did when I walked in on you, admiring the watch you *stole* from the man on the pier."

Ollie's deep gasp, at that moment, seems to be the result of pain more than surprise. Her face is set in a terrible rictus. With every word of our exchange, DeSant pushes her arm up, deaf to her cries. Ollie's protests, however, are almost drowned by the continuing whimpers from the terrified Maureen.

DeSant, however, ignores them both with a "fuck me, you're a pair of noisy bitches." The only upside is that his anger is now fully directed at me. As he comes closer, he plunks Ollie on a chair to my right. Maureen, meekly, takes a chair to my left, momentarily ignored.

I can smell his cologne as DeSant then lowers his bulk, not two inches from my face. In the silence, I hear deep sighs coming from Ollie as Maureen lapses into silence.

"Admiring it. Give me a break," he intones after a few

seconds, his temper now under control. As he hovers closer, I am sure he is going to hit me. "You make me sound like a villain in a James Bond movie. I wasn't *admiring* it, you useless old broad." Again, DeSant's voice turns indignant. He seems to alternate between whiny self-pity and murderous rage.

"I took it out to get it ready for the guy who's gonna take it off my hands. No use wasting his time or mine when he finally gets here. Fuck me, didn't anybody ever teach you to wait for a *come in*, before entering? Tell that low-rent husband of yours to buy you some manners, will you?

"Look, I'm not a bad person, honest," he continues in a measured tone of voice after a few seconds. It is as if the man who spewed out insults a foot from my face has disappeared, to be replaced by the affable host he prides himself to be.

"That thing with him...with Xavi? It was an impulse. Bad judgment. Call it what you will. I panicked. I couldn't take the chance he'd recognized the watch. Honest, I'm not a murderer. I had the memorial, didn't I? I swear to you, if things weren't about to go south, I'd help Annie, too."

"Not a bad guy? Then turn yourself in. It was an accident, you say. That baby is about to grow up without a father. Xavi's family deserves some closure."

"Enough. That's enough out of you. Another word, and you'll be sorry. No, not you, your two pals. And it'll be on you. Go ahead, keep talking, see what'll happen," he adds. "You know wh..."

Without finishing the phrase, he steps away from me a few paces, and then, slowly and with great deliberation, he slaps Ollie as casually as you'd flick a fly away. And with enough force to his backhand to make her head bounce back.

I see her body slump into the chair. She's not unconscious, but all the fight seems to be gone from her. Next to me, the silent Maureen begins to cry loudly again.

As I lapse into mute horror, DeSant moves towards

his desk. The same place where I found him, deep in the contemplation of the watch. Funny thing, I'm pretty sure if he had just put it back in the open drawer, I would've not even noticed. But when we locked eyes, I knew. I knew right then he was the Naples Pier thief.

I couldn't help betraying that I knew any more than I could hold back the words that came out of me then. "It was you!"

"That's more like it. Nice and quiet. Hey, you, crazy. Stop it," he orders in Maureen's direction. Her sobs have now become a steady stream of mumbled words. When his words fail to silence her, however, he rolls his eyes, shrugs his shoulders, and sits behind the desk again.

"I'm telling you," obviously aggrieved, "If there's one thing I won't mind, it is being done with all the rich old crazies in this damn town. "

I let out the breath I didn't know I'd held. I was afraid Maureen would be the next one at the receiving end of one of his violence, but he turns his back on her as he continues to address me.

"So, it's ciao, Naples, for me. And you, all you got to do is wait a little longer until my friend shows up. God knows what's keeping him. I guess I should call him my fence, right?" DeSant continues, almost chatty. "Such a distrustful guy. Professional hazard, I bet. He wouldn't meet me anywhere else. It was either here or at my house.

"And no sense in having the little woman," he chuckles, as if at a private joke, "asking why he's driving the Beemer away. Seeing as she's not coming with, don't you think? And then, hello, Maldives or whatever spot can use a good restaurant. A little too hot in the kitchen these days.

"You know what I mean, right? You were in the business, too," he adds with a wink of complicity.

"You owe money, right and left. And word's starting

to get out. You owe everybody in Naples," I pipe in, incensed by that wink. As if Manny and I had ever been in his thieving league.

"You knew?" I nod yes, in answer, a little embarrassed. I knew, and I never put it together.

"How is it that everybody in this damned town knows everybody else's business, you tell me. But you're right. There are a few produce bills unpaid, a matter of a late payroll, and a couple of mortgages behind. A few inconveniences."

"I'd been planning to decamp for a while, true," he adds with a deep sigh. "But now...well, now I'll just have to go a little farther. Somewhere, where there are no extra whatchamacallits with the good old US of A."

For a few blessed seconds, DeSant stops talking. In the sudden silence, we can still hear Maureen whimpering softly. He then checks his watch and sighs.

"He should be here any moment. Not much longer. In the meanwhile, well, I'm so sorry."

The surreal aspect of the moment doubles when I realize DeSant's apology is sincere. Striking Ollie, the violence against us, it has all slipped his mind. Filed under "I'm not a bad guy," no doubt.

He then moves to rip up several tablecloths. His fists, I note, have no trouble tearing up the heavy fabric after an initial stab with a pair of sharp scissors. Scissors and fists, I note silently, with increasing dread.

"My apologies, so sorry," he repeats. He redoubles my ties, anchoring my ankles to the legs of the chair. But he's especially harsh, I notice when tying Ollie's arms. Something in Ollie's bearing has really touched a nerve in Philippe DeSant.

"Don't worry, though. Tuesday morning is just around the corner. I'm sure you girls will be fine. Your phone," he says to Ollie then, once he's done securing the knots. "Quick.

Don't make me have to reach into your pocket."

Despite the pain that casts a greyish tint on her face, she now looks ready to murder him. On her left cheek, an angry red welt already marks her skin. Eventually, however, and with great reluctance, she points to her right pocket with her head.

When DeSant gets to Maureen, he stares at her for a few seconds, gingerly considering the mumbling woman before him, now convulsed with dry retching.

"You're not going to puke all over me, right?" he asks, patting the pockets of her jeans. Just then, as if in answer, Maureen drops to the floor at his feet.

"What the fuuuuuck…"

"It's arched, it's French, it's Fifth. Ohhh, the pain! Somebody, please help me! Help!" Maureen cries from the floor, her hands still free, desperately stabbing her stomach.

"Don't just stand there!" In her concern, Ollie tries to jump from the chair, a move that wrenches her arms forward in a way that's too horrible to watch.

"She may be suffering from something serious," she manages to whimper despite the pain. "She had a bad accident just a few days ago."

"No shit, if she keeps throwing herself around like that. So, you're the one," DeSant adds, poking Maureen with a tentative foot. "I remember you now. Thanks to you, the cops know I was at the pier, too. Not waiting for them to finish sniffing around. They've already come around here once."

Maureen, meanwhile, continues to writhe on the floor, her complaints so loud that I can barely hear DeSant and Ollie. "It's arched, it's French, it's the Fifth. Ohhh, the paaaaain!"

I'm beginning to grow seriously concerned. Can the strain of a dangerous situation trigger some kind of mental breakdown? Maybe Ollie is right. Perhaps Maureen is suffering some awful consequence to her fall, only making itself felt now, aggravated by the stress of the last half hour.

As if by unspoken agreement, for a few heartbeats, the three of us stare down at Maureen, thrashing on the floor. And then, an almost flowery sensation floods my mind. I could swear I smell something green. Hope is green, isn't it? A burst of hope warms my rigid muscles. A feeling that banishes my fears for Maureen, for Ollie, for myself. Hope, eternal hope.

Because I've just realized that in those same few moments, a wonderful, distant sound intruded into the silent office. Sirens, a multitude of sirens, coming nearer. Police sirens that finally stop right outside the arched, uniquely decorated entrance of Á Toute Á L'Heure, the French landmark on Fifth Avenue.

CHAPTER NINE

MO

Don't let it not be said, ever, that the Martin women are made of flimsy stuff. We were tested. And like the very best of mulberry silks, we came through the trial whole. Our heads held high and our coiffures in place.

Mom's dementia; any number of childhood accidents of Trey's and Molly's; Brian, gone in a matter of weeks; Giancarlo struck by a heart attack in his office; theft at the hand of a man who had sworn to protect me: the list of horrors life has thrown my way is a long one. Whose isn't? Who has lived to reach my age? To that catalogue, however, I will add the sight of that maniac torturing my brave sister, ready to do us any sort of unspeakable horrors to us next.

Even after a longer than usual yoga session this morning, which allowed much time for reflection, I cannot begin to fathom how I ever consider him — the Unmentionable One, forevermore — an attractive man. Ollie would shake her head and give me one of her "told you so, Mo." A painful as it is warranted reminder in this occasion.

She is still abed, of course, where I carefully helped her find a comfortable position last night, a mound of pillows cocooning her sling. I expect her to remain there all day today.

She won't ever admit it, but I saw mortal fear haunting my sister's eyes yesterday. It was an unusually meek and quiet Ollie who was wheeled into the ambulance. Attracted by the emergency lights bouncing off the nearby facades, a mob of onlookers crowded around us, phones in hand, as a fitful rain began to fall. I hope they all had their expensive clothes ruined, those vultures.

As I mounted the Naples EMT vehicle with the aid of a masculine hand—I so appreciate a courteous man in a uniform—uppermost on my mind was the need to spare my sister any photographic indignities. Thank heavens, the crew wasted no time in leaving the scene of the crime. Yes, the crime.

And then we were zooming off. That same technician, a very fine representative of his department, I must say, was kind enough to explain the function of the blood pressure cuff as he used it on my sister. This was a distraction that went some way toward relieving my worries. We had barely had time to exchange names—it turns out his name is Brian, too—when Ollie groaned.

"Really, Mo? Here and now?" With those words bravely whispered under her breath, I knew then my sister was back in form, the champion that she is.

I'm happy to report that at the hospital, they decided not to keep Ollie overnight. We had to wait an inordinate amount of time, I thought, for two victims of a criminal maniac. A wait at the ER is always a good sign, at least, according to my Dr. Molly. Proof whatever ails you is not a true emergency. At least, so she kept repeating when I placed frantic calls to both of my children.

Calls made on my life-saving phone if I'm allowed a bit of bragging today.

Still, Ollie will be wearing a cumbersome contraption on her arm for quite a few days. She was also sent home with various prescriptions and a list of recommended orthopedists. Given my sister's grit, however, I see her turning the corner soon.

In fact, even as I tucked her into bed last night, a mountain of my best embroidered pillows propping her arm, Ollie informed me she's determined to keep her date with Helen Stratemeyer. Our local celebrity author has agreed to "mentor" Ollie.

The Universe only knows what that is all about. My sister being mentored by a writer. I'll just be grateful if they don't end up killing each other. Extremely grateful.

As I remain today. Grateful, Universe, that you spared me my sister. Grateful you spared Betty and her kind, brave heart, too. Grateful I was here, today, to greet the dawn with a loud, "Good morning, sun!" Grateful my mind and soul are whole, all in one piece, despite the time spent in the clutches of that madman.

I'll show him, see if I don't. I will be double damned if I ever acknowledge his restaurant, let alone his name, when I finally get around to serving the chocolate mousse. Felipe, the creator, of course. Xavi, most assuredly. But that monster's name shall never cross my lips again. And that, to borrow a phrase, is all I have to say about that.

***

"Isn't that right, Bertie?" In response to my query, he runs to the front door. I have just enough time to remove a couple of trays from the oven, and there it is. The insistent ringing of the doorbell.

I wonder who it is? I am assuming the Naples media has broadcasted the details of our ordeal. Such a juicy story: "Local ladies defeat criminal mastermind." I can almost hear the anchor reading that bit. I wonder? Should I forward the Naples Daily News a couple of pictures of myself? Just in case they decide to use them in later editions. Ollie's, too, of course.

I remain, of course, ignorant of what's been said in the media. Few things disturb my santosha in the morning more than the intrusion of the outside world. Never a fan of early morning news shows, ever, not that our set is of any use these days. And the Naples News was, again, unreadable this morning.

The doorbell rings for a second time as I test the goodies for doneness. Along with my yoga and gratitude journaling, I did some serious early morning baking. If I know my fellow yogis, for one, they will be descending on us soon. As soon as common sense and good taste allows. Which in the case of Amy Martino, it won't be too long, naturellement.

It's been a similar story with the phone. Again, my life-saving phone. I've fielded calls all morning, mainly from the rest of the family. As for Molly and Trey, they wouldn't let us go to bed without taking an actual look at the two of us through that thingamajig app.

"I need to see you, Mama Bear. Aunt Ollie, too. With my own eyes," insisted Trey, his voice wavering. And they say women are emotional.

I also returned a call from Betty, asking for details from the hospital visit, before finally turning in for the night. We're comrades in arms. The three of us tested and true and ready for battle. "*Allons enfants de la patrie!*" Although, in this case, it was more *allons mesdames de la patrie.* "Coming!" I add as the doorbell rings for a third time.

CARMEN CINTRON, NPD

When the front door finally opens, I take a quick look-see around. Could've sworn I heard a few refrains of that song everybody learns in French 1. Whatever. Instead, Maureen sends a sunny smile in my direction, grabs my hand, and pulls me right in like we're old pals.

Which I guess we are, given what's happened. Civilians are always happy to see police after we've saved their bacon. No matter how many times we screw up. Which is plenty. Facts of life, both.

I can't believe it's been a week to the day since Alexander and I first visited this place on the trail of that stolen watch. Like the last time, Maureen is wearing one of her fancy mu-mus. I bet she and my Aunt Carmen, Junior — not to be confused with Aunt Carmen, Senior — could have a lot to talk about when it comes to clothes.

All huge fans of fancy get-ups, in fact. Tía Carmen, Junior; tía Carmen, Senior; tía Carmina; tía Carmela; tía Carme; tía Carmiña, married to the old Cuban *gallego*; tía Carmenchu; tía Carmelita, the extra-religious one, always wearing the scapulary of Our Lady of Mount Carmel; tía Carmy and our most recent acquisition, Tía Karma, formerly Carlos Rossi, who in their own words, "dropped the shame, embraced the Carmen and is never looking back."

Like the last time, too, Maureen is shadowed by that weird-ass mutt of theirs. I notice in a corner a chewed-up copy of the newspaper, still in its wrapper, on top of a pile of several equally mangled copies.

"Bertie's not happy with the delivery person," she throws my way as she sees me eyeing the pile. "Perhaps there's some criminal ring involved in the newspaper delivery. You may want to check that out. Otherwise, I can't figure out why he's acting this way."

One look at *Bertie,* and I could give her the why. That is one crazy-looking dog. Ese perro está más loco que las cabras, as my mami would say. Why are island goats crazier than other species is a story I've never heard. Maybe it's just Boricua goats that are particularly nuts.

Again, as during my last visit, I'm offered coffee and scones. I pass on the pastries. I'm not a fan, but I do grab a couple of warm oatmeal cookies which arrive on a fancy plate, accompanied by a cloth napkin. A real cup and saucer, too, no mug. Who knew a regular oatmeal cookie could taste so good?

While I busy myself chewing, Maureen turns and asks, her voice fresh like a morning birdsong: "To what do I owe the honor — Oh, no! I forgot to call you! I really meant to call, but it slipped my mind.

"The taping's been moved to tomorrow, Tuesday. I hope you still can come. You *did* you had some PTO coming. Of course, it would've helped if I had called you to let you know, earlier," she finishes with a giggle, her voice as fresh as the first songbird of dawn.

"It's fine, no worries. I'm not here for…" Now, it's my turn to be taken back. "Wait, what? You mean to say you're going through with the taping tomorrow?"

"We most assuredly are, yes. Aren't we, Bertie?"

"That's some feisty mama you got there, dude," it's all I can say, looking down at el loco de Bertie. Hearing his name, he moves on to try to hump my ankle. I move him aside with a swift kick. A baby one.

"I didn't think we were going through with it. I'm on my way to the gym," I add, pointing to my clothes. "I just thought I'd stop by and see how you two were doing. That was some stunt you pulled yesterday."

"Well, I don't want to brag, but yes, I'd like to think I saved the day. Ooooh, you really like the cookies, I see. So many people are not fans of raisins."

"Mm…mm," is all I can manage as I nod my head.

"A mix of granulated and brown sugars and plenty of butter, incorporated with a lot of beating. Or have a friend bake them for you," she adds with another peal of what I'll be calling "light morning laughter" from now on.

She then drops down and carefully places two cookies

next to Bertie, who moves in like a starving prisoner. Before I can answer — like I'm ever going near an oven if I can help it — a series of tentative thumps comes from the wide hallway to the right of us, where the staircase is located.

A few seconds later, Mrs. Howard enters the kitchen. Her arm is strapped close to her torso. At first, she seems the same Ollie. The same stern, take-no-prisoners look to her features. And then she turns towards me, and my breath catches a little bit in my throat. There's a vulnerability in that wide, blue gaze that wasn't there last time we spoke.

It may pass, or it may not. Even rookie police sometimes find it difficult to accept there's bad guys out there, always on the lookout to hurt others. It's particularly difficult to accept there's men who would maim women simply because they can. Because they're stronger.

I feel for her, I really do, so I gently say, "Call me Cici, please," when she greets me with a short nod of her head and a curt "Good morning, detective."

OLLIE

I don't know if I'm at all comfortable with this new "call me See-see for Cici" attitude of my erstwhile interrogator, but I nod again in acknowledgement of the offer. I cannot help but notice Mo has taken to calling her by the nickname, like the proverbial house on fire. It's all "Another cookie, See-See?" as I make my way slowly into the kitchen.

Personally, I'm still waiting for an apology on behalf of the NPD. An apology I noted went missing from our last meeting with her partner. An apology which would be totally in order, given how we have solved "The Case of the Missing Watch." Not to mention landed them a murderer.

But let that be as it may. Don't let it ever be said Ollie Howard cannot let bygones be bygones. So, I continue to move in dignified silence, feeling every one of my years, towards the stool Mo has moved away from the counter for me.

She has also set a plate of scones right before it and one of my favorite mugs "Librarians — The Original Search Engines." It's a measure of my diminished state that her fussiness only brings a small grimace to my face.

My sister then moves to prepare my first cup of the day just the way I like it. Very dark, a splash of cream, one sugar. I do stop her, however, as she begins to slice the cinnamon scone into quarters.

"Thank you, my dear. I can take it from here," I say instead, trying not to roll my eyes in response to her mothering. Mo turns to the detective next and refills her cup — one of the Limoges, I see — with a wide smile on her carefully made-up face.

A session of yoga under her belt, no doubt another hour of scribbling, and a full complement of makeup. And the sun has barely peeped over the horizon. I'm about to remark on that, too, but I opt for peace instead. Peace and plenty of caffeine are the only ways to meet a day like today, oh, yes.

"You were saying…" Mo continues, moving the plate of oatmeal cookies forward. Those are my mom's oatmeal breakfast cookies. And if my memory of Mo's usual quantities when baking is correct, our visitor has already eaten nearly a dozen.

Somehow, the fact that she appreciates Mom's baking traditions and that she is not given to whining about the inclusion of raisins makes me feel a little better disposed towards Detective "We'll See About Cici" Cintron.

I lean forward as she continues to recount facts, I could have worked out for myself. But again, I keep my peace. "The theft of the watch was just opportunism, of course.

"DeSant had no previous designs on the owner, he claims. He simply gave in on the impulse as he recognized the value of the item at his feet. The guy has a thing for expensive watches. Expensive anythings, apparently.

"It was Bianchi's very bad luck that he went looking for the missing schedule on his own, and he found it. Right there in the same drawer as the watch. And with that, he was marked for murder. DeSant says he thought Bianchi had recognized the stolen item and was just being cagy, waiting to blackmail him, maybe."

"*Ladrón juzga por su condición*, as my grandma has it. A thief judges others by his condition. You're a criminal. Others must be, too. DeSant swears Bianchi was just waiting for the right moment to demand his cut once he recognized the date inscribed on the back of the watch.

"I suppose the owner can credit his amazing lack of taste for the item's recovery. It would've been difficult for that *person* – I use the term generously – to explain how he came to have the engraved watch in his possession."

In response, the two figures before me simply shake their heads as if in agreement. There is no accounting for the tackiness of some of the world's richest people, I'd like to add, but instead, I produce an unknown fact. Unknown by the police, I'm delighted to note.

"Still, we were there, in the kitchen when he came back. It didn't look like Xavier recognized the import of the date. If he even saw it. Or maybe, like so many young people, he didn't read the newspaper."

The detective reaches for yet another cookie with a "There's that" as I continue with more vigor. "But how was it that the police showed up right at the right moment when we needed help? Did you have him under surveillance?"

"The minute you ladies identified him as being present on the pier when the theft occurred, he went on our radar. He knew that. He also knew we'd be getting to the damage to his car sooner than later. No doubt that's why he was in such a hurry to get out of town. By the way, that's one Naples fence that won't be operating around here, either."

"But the credit for your rescue belongs to somebody else," she continues with a grin, wiping the cookie crumbles from her not-unattractive features. She does have a very pleasing smile, I'll concede. And lovely curls, Mo is right.

"Your sister hit 911 while having a spectacular meltdown. And she placed a call to my cell while she was at it." For a good thirty seconds, it's all silence in the kitchen while I stare, slightly agape, at my Mo. I can feel bits of scone falling onto the plate.

"Good show, Maureen! Brava!" I finally exclaim, grabbing another pastry to replace the one now crumbled before me.

I am sure I can be forgiven the slight note of amazement that colors my voice. Mo, my sweet, clueless sister. Mo, who makes me worry about her future without me, if I must be perfectly honest. Mo, whose knowledge of detecting methods would fit into one of those teeny concoctions of feathers and sparkly *stuff* she calls her Lieber purses.

And with that one, another thought appears, fast on its heels. "*Wondering if there was anything I had left undone. I could think of nothing. With a shake of the head, I passed out and closed the door behind me.*" I've re-read the Christie passage so many times in the last few days I can recite it from memory.

"It was the moment when Xavier came back to the kitchen during the mousse lesson," I try to explain to my confused audience. "DeSant's face said it all. Would he be leaving *anything undone* if he allowed Xavier to walk away? Could he trust that the young man hadn't seen the date? Or realize later what he'd seen? That's the look that kept me fixated on the novel!

"If only…if only I'd remembered sooner," I finish with a sigh. In response, Mo pats my hand as I continue to stare in distress at my breakfast plate.

"Well, yeah," our young visitor agrees doubtfully, at length. The detective is obviously unaware of the Christie reference. Kids these days have no knowledge of the classics. "There is that, too. Had he recognized it later, Bianchi could've simply grabbed the phone, called us, and sat back and waited for the reward."

While she helps herself to one last oatmeal cookie, Mo and I stare at each other for a couple of breaths. "The reward!" We both exclaim, almost in unison.

"That's right! We almost forgot about it," Mo adds. Needlessly, I feel. Small memory lapses are totally understandable, given our recent ordeal.

"That was the first reason we went into the investigation. The reward for the watch. And then we go and forget about it," she insists with a distressing lack of tact.

"Well, the reward and the clearing of my name. Or have you forgotten the bit about *shiny things* on the pier?" I applaud myself, if only mentally, for refraining from casting pointed stares in our visitor's direction.

As if struck by amnesia, the detective smiles happily, dusting her hands. "Boy, Maureen, those are some amazing cookies. Then it gives me great pleasure to say, kudos, girlfriend. That the reason you went to the restaurant yesterday was the reward, I mean," Detective Cici clarifies, emphasizing the word ever-so-slightly.

"The rule about rewards is that the person who claims it must have performed the services knowing of the offer. In this case, it was only information leading to the return. No conviction was necessary. So, yes, three lady bounty hunters. You didn't just find the watch by accident."

"But we were looking for Betty. We didn't stop there —" begins my ever-innocent sister.

"I'm gonna stop you right there, chica. Think very

carefully about what you're gonna be telling the insurance agency. Right, Mrs. H.?" the detective asks in my direction. "I have to go now," she adds, while placing her coffee cup, with great care, in the sink behind her.

"I leave your sister in your very capable hands," she finishes, throwing a brief wink in my direction.

I stare at her for the count of three. "You can count on me," I finally shoot back. "Cici."

***

Before we do anything else today, before retrieving Coral, which is still parked in front of the Tutti Frutti, there is a visit we are honor bound to make. Mo makes a quick phone call. My sister, her bossy pants firmly in place today, insists she'll drive. I am in no state to attempt to walk, even if it's just a few blocks, she insists.

Boy, call 911 once, and you are Head Girl forever. While I agree with her in theory about my momentary disability, I must add I foresee difficult days ahead should she continue to display that Mama Bear trait of hers that Dr. Molly and Trey find so amusingly charming. When it's not directed at them, of course.

As always, Betty is early. And like the last time, she waits by the door of the Tortoni, under the wide arcaded entrance of the building. Rare for her, however, today, she is dressed in a cream linen pants and jacket outfit that wouldn't look out of place in her old office.

Our first greetings over, we lapse into silence. Betty's face has regained its usual serenity. Our friend is a study in Zen. In marked contrast to Mo and me, I'll also admit. We bickered, at some length, over the best space to park on Broad Street, but only because my sister is unusually headstrong this afternoon.

All the more interesting, then, is to remember the moral outrage with which she confronted that man just last night. Brava, Betty!

We continue to stare at each other for another couple of heartbeats as customers stream into the café behind us. And then, we come together into a wordless circle of heads, only to spring apart with sheepish grins a few seconds later.

"How are you holding up, Ollie?"

"It is good to be alive," is my only answer. What else is there to say? The days we are apportioned are a gift. I have long known that.

Inside, the Tortoni is a hive of colors and voices. Orders to go are called out while a couple of young waitresses circulate with trays. I believe the correct term is wait staff these days.

Off in the corner, usually occupied by Mish-Mish and Dita, two tables have been pushed together. Gathered tightly around them, a gaggle of squealing teens snaps photos of what seems to be every item on offer at the café. To the side, Anne Bianchi is unloading even more treats onto the tables from a tray propped against her stomach.

She espies us and puts the last plate down with a definite thump. "Let me know if there's still something left on the menu you didn't get," she laughs as she ambles towards us.

Waddle would be the more apt term. Her pregnancy is so near to term, I am shocked Octavio and Brad would allow her anywhere near the floor of the Tortoni. "I couldn't sit on my butt. Not today, not after the detectives called," she says when she reaches our side as if answering the concern that was surely visible on my face.

She then leans forward awkwardly and tries to put her arms around the three of us. "He didn't get away with it. The son of a bitch didn't get away with it. Hashtag justice for Xavi," she whispers with glee. In her devilish grin, I can already see the ferocious parent she is going to be.

"Annie, what did we agree?" That is Octavio calling out from behind the counter. By his side, Brad looks as alarmed as I probably did on first seeing Anne still waiting on customers.

"I know, I know. I'm giving my tray to Marcie, see?" she yells back with a shake of her head, handing the utensil to one of the wait staff. "Here I go, taking off my apron. Finishing right now. Heading to the door, see that?" she cries out as she finally heads out. "I'll see you at home, lovies!"

"If anything happens…"

"You'll be the first to know, no worries. Not having this baby without you," Xavier's young widow exclaims in farewell, closing the door of the Tortoni behind her to the echoes of its elegant three-toned bell.

Turns out the family knows about the arrest, but our visit is not over, so we approach the counter next. Both men come from behind it during a momentary lull of activity. Brad then bows deeply in our direction, a curiously old-fashioned salute. Quite charming, I must say. "We are forever in your debt, ladies. Thank you for bringing some peace into our lives."

He then returns to his post by the cash register while Octavio moves us towards the opposite corner of the café, slightly screened from the rest of the room by a bank of potted azaleas in bloom. Behind the display, Dita and Mish-Mish lounge serenely. As if they know today is a special day, they raise their elegant heads with alert, doggy eyes and, I could swear, a couple of smiles in our direction.

Still silent, Octavio then takes turns lifting our hands — mine first — in both of his, bringing it to his lips, and planting a kiss on each. With a sharp pang of sorrow, I am reminded of Xavier bowing deeply over Mo's hand the last time we saw him. "Now, don't go on and forget me, Miss Maureen. I expect you to visit me often."

For a few seconds, Octavio's head remains bowed,

almost as if in prayer. It doesn't take me that long to notice he has lost some of his old Hollywood glamour. He has lost the athletic posture that was so like his nephew's. His hair appears a little less shiny, greyer, too. Deep wrinkles circle his eyes when he finally lifts his gaze.

"*Gracias, mil gracias.* With all my heart, thank you," is all he says. Then, bowing his head again as if talking to himself, he asks simply, "How do you do it?!"

"You fold your arms, and you breathe deeply," Mo answers at length, in her softest tone of voice. "And you remember to exhale. And then you tell yourself, you will power through it, somehow. You never get over it, but you survive. And, in time, perhaps even find a measure of joy again."

I wouldn't presume, of course, to give advice on the loss of a child, but I have known sorrow, of course. And so, I find my voice next. "I only met your son once, but of one thing, I am certain. Those who love us want us to be happy, even when they're gone. And we're only a call away," I finish, pointing at the familiar shape of a cell phone in his apron pocket.

Next thing, I'm entering my number among his contacts while Betty, still silent, holds one of his hands in two of hers. A soothing "tsk, tsk" is the only sound coming from her lips, almost as if calming a fretful child.

Just like that, our visit to the Café Tortoni is over. Another round of pats for Mish-Mish and Dita, another gentlemanly bow from Brad, Octavio now back by his side, still staring somewhere off in the distance. And then we close the doors behind us.

This time, we know we'll be back soon. And we'll find a second home within its walls when we do.

BETTY

The rain is still falling just as I drive into the garage. The showers began just as I was parking on Fifth Avenue after the unexpected visit to the Tortoni. I guess the collection of umbrellas is now permanently stowed in my car and my tote bag, in expectation of the summer downpours — the way I once used to carry CTA tokens in my pockets — makes me a real Floridian now.

"Over here!" Manny shouts as soon as he spots me. At this side, Freddy raises his head with that handsome smile of his. If I know my husband, they'll while away what is left of the afternoon, happily working the squad logistics, the two of them looking like a pair of generals engrossed by their task.

I grin back and gesture towards the bedroom in turn. I'm pretty sure by the time I reach the door, the two will have forgotten about me. Just as I'm sure, Manny won't be feeling totally at peace for the foreseeable future unless he knows where I am at every moment.

He told me as much this morning, already apologizing for it. "Just for a few days, okay, Betts? Text me and text me often," he pleaded, first thing this morning.

I undress with a sigh and jump in the shower. There are days in July, I swear, when three showers are not enough, dry skin be damned. Once done, I head outside with another glance at the guys. There they are, heads nearly touching, peering at the laptop.

I step outside to find a clear afternoon. The sky over the pool has that just washed tint of blue that follows the rain, a sort of faded denim. It arches over the long sweep of sands that have been darkened to deep umber by the showers.

The mob of beach goers is back in force, I notice, opening the tropical floral print chairs we all bought, at a discount, in the same store, readying themselves to say goodbye to the sun as it eventually begins its descent towards the dark pearl grey horizon. Maybe today will be it. Maybe today will be a green flash day. I hope so for their sake.

I busy myself drying a couple of the backyard chairs to regain my sense of balance. Of course, to call this spot a *backyard* is a bit of a private joke. When the realtor first showed me the house, this area reminded me of that poster I once saw at the Art Institute but couldn't afford. Me, the frustrated Art History major who had to choose a more *sensible* career.

Who could've guessed decades later, I'd be living in one of Hockney's "Splash" paintings?

As I go about walking around the pool, straightening the chaise lounges chairs — wicker Chac-mools — I realize that thinking of the outside living area in *backyard* terms, like remembering the CTA tokens, is another throwback to my childhood. When every three-flat we ever lived in had a postage-stamp square of sod behind it, planted with a couple of tomato plants that ever-hopeful Ma would buy each spring.

Thoughts of Ma have been running through my mind, even more than usual, ever since last night. I think from heaven, she reached out and made me braver than I ever thought I could be. She, who left the Appalachia with just a suitcase in one hand and three-year-old me in the other, ready to seek a new life for us in the big city.

I also realize that fussing over the linens for tomorrow's dinner allows me to focus on something other than that uneasy mix of anticipation and anxiety that's making me queasy. Doesn't all anticipation cause queasiness? I suppose in some lucky folks it doesn't.

Mine is compounded by lingering shock and sadness. It weighed on my soul visiting Octavio, even if it was to bring the news Xavi's murderer had been caught. But Maureen was correct. He, Anne, Brad, they all deserved to know. While we had no way of knowing the detectives in the case would call them early with news of the arrest, I'm still happy I agreed to accompany them. What an unspeakable horror it must be to go through life not knowing who is responsible for the death of your child.

***

Nice linens, starched, no less, are available in the outside cupboard, but when Manny and I finally sit down for our usual evening drinks, it's paper napkins and small plastic bowls to go with our "standing order," as he calls it. A glass of wine for me — red or white, depending on the season — and a plain beer for him.

"I bet you anything that Brad and Octavio don't know what a plastic bowl looks like," I giggle, pushing the cashews towards my husband.

"The Tortoni guys? Hey, you want to invite them for tomorrow night? No problem at all unless the pregnant girl is a vegan. I'll just throw a few more steaks and lobsters on the barbie, mate."

"That's gotta be the worst Australian accent in recorded history, you. No, we'll have them over another time. Then we can meet the baby. It's probably too last minute an invite. Too soon for Octavio, too."

We sip in easy silence for a few more minutes. I wouldn't want to share the sunset hour with anybody else. Over our heads, the sun begins its descent in a sky that seems glazed, like an antique ceramic. A slight evening breeze ripples the surface of the pool into a treasure chest of golden coins.

"Doesn't that color remind you of the Chinese vases at the Art Institute?" I ask eventually, pointing up. "And how when we first got married, we'd go there on the free days as a treat? Because we had no money for anything else."

"I remember being broke. And the dates. The art, are you serious? Over my head," he replies, with a whistle and an upturned hand. "And speaking of money, it's all set, then?

That was the last meeting with the finance guys?"

"All set," I agree. "I need to start thinking of hiring people, of course, but everything is in place. And it's a good place. The Counting on You Foundation will be up and running as of next month. That's a good name you came up with."

"I had to redeem myself, you mean. Who would've thought I'd go through life as Manny, the Brats Boss of Chicago? Had I known how things would turn out when Ma bankrolled us, I would've put marketing experts in charge earlier," he guffaws.

I stare at my husband's grey eyes for a while longer, and what I see in them makes my heart sing. Gone is the anxiety that plagued me. Life is a dangerous road, filled with dark turns and evil people, but with the right companion, it is a blessed path.

"Here's to us," I don't give Manny a chance to complete the toast as I rush along. "And perdition to our enemies,"

"Don't, not today," my husband pleads, his gaze suddenly serious. "When I think of what could've happened. Tough guy, picking on women half his size." His tone is stern, but I notice he blinks a couple of tears from the corner of his eyes.

"Then don't go there, like the kids used to say," I answer lightly. I feel a burst of energy run through me with those words. I realize then that DeSant had not achieved his ends. I was not afraid then. Thanks, Ma! I will not be afraid now. Whatever comes my way from now on, I will prevail.

"Not with this gorgeous sea, this beautiful sunset before us," I continue after a second, waving my hands around us. "*Oh, the days dwindle down to a precious few...And these few precious days I'll spend with you,*" I hum next. "I remember how Ma would sing along when Sarah Vaughn came on the radio."

Still staring into his eyes, I leave my seat and come

around the table. "Alexa, play *September Song*. Come on, you," I say then, giving Manny's hand a small tug as the musical strains fill the space around us.

Behind us, the sun finally sparkles one last time as it dips into the ocean to the sound of my husband's delighted laughter. "One, two, three... one, two, three. Easy there, Betts."

Not too much later, Manny follows me into the house. And the rest, as they say, is history.

CHAPTER TEN

CATALINA CINTRON, NPD

"Here I go again. Gotta watch those cookies don't turn into a habit," I chuckle to myself as I approach the giant umbrella tree that shadows pretty much the front of the cottage. What is that thing called, anyway?

The cottage looks different today. A place that holds a couple of easily overlooked treasures inside. Gotta hand it to them. These two are two feisty mujeres. I wonder if many people my age realize how brave most older women are on any given day.

The property is a mess, still. That hasn't changed from our first visit. You feel you'll need a machete one of these days to make it to the front door. But it's a lovely, homey mess. And an expensive one, I remind myself, despite the decaying garage, the much-needed roofing, and yep, there it is, right on time, the demented guard dog.

"Good day, Detective Cici. Right this way." If not bubbly, like Maureen's, Mrs. H.'s manner toward me has thawed somewhat. She invites me in with one hand while keeping one leg extended, the better to keep the cray-cray mutt away from the doorway and a dash for freedom.

Bertie's got that look, you know. Like the minute he

hits the street, he'd be off, and he wouldn't be found ni en los centros espiritistas. One of abuela's favorite sayings. Grandma being a huge fan of those spiritualist seances at the Jersey botánicas that offer to get you in touch with "the Other Side."

Now that I think about it, that's another point towards explaining the feels I'm developing over here. Abuela and Maureen would get along like the two gandules in a pod. I chortle under my breath at the image and then put my most professional face on, thinking of the reason that brings me back here today.

My mom's recipe is now available over the Internet for the whole world to taste and appreciate. How about that?

"And good day to you, too, Mrs. Howard," I respond with a small bow as I follow her into the wide porch. I have noticed she's not inviting me to call her by her first name today, either. "Hey there, Bertie. Good to see you, too. Feisty as ever, I see," I add, keeping my hands wisely to myself and away from his snapping jaws.

"His name is Bert, just Bert," Mrs. H. responds, the temperature dropping a few degrees. "Please don't fall into my sister's habits of infantilizing him."

I say nothing—I've learned some conversations, like walls, are best going around—and follow her into the cottage. Today, the big table that's usually in the small dining room, usually covered in files and journals, has been moved forward towards the front windows.

I can also see two strangers setting up some equipment. One's a skinny white guy, thin enough to give Alexander some competition, with a mop of orange hair. He looks strangely familiar, but I can't place him. The other person is a young woman in a flowered hijab. While I can't see her hair, of course, the minute she lifts her face with a shy smile, it's as if I was looking in a mirror. She could be my younger sister.

My much prettier younger sister.

Between her and Doritos-orange-hair guy, there's a cell phone on a tripod and what looks to be some sophisticated lighting equipment. *¡Ay, bendito!* This is really gonna happen. My squeaky voice is about to be sent into the Big Bad Web. I've always thought I sound like Minnie Mouse on tape.

And with those crazy thoughts, I give in to what I'm really feeling: nerves, plain nerves. *Do I look okay? Should I have worn something more formal? Is the squad gonna give me untold shit for this? What have I gotten myself into?* Before I can work myself into a heart attack, however, I hear a voice from the nearby kitchen.

"Darling Cici, you made it! Namaste, my dear," Maureen accompanies her words with a bow over folded hands. "May the light of your kind spirit guide us all today."

"Cici, these are Shaggy and Ayesha, our techie wonders," she adds, pointing unnecessarily in their direction. At least now I know where that memory came from, a cartoon ditty now scampering through my head.

"Pleasure to meet you, Ayesha, Shaggy?"

"Go right ahead, Cici," he answers, focusing on the tripod instead, while Ayesha nods happily by his side.

Encouraged by the good vibes all around me—even Mrs. H. is looking kindly on the scene—I take a deep breath as I cross behind the alcove and take my place next to Maureen. To hell with nerves. What is it that tía Carmenchu always says? "*¿Pa'tras? Ni pa' coger impulso.*" She's right. No sense in looking back, even if it's to get a running start.

"Ready, ladies? Three, two, one…action!"

MO

"And that, my lovies, is how you prepare arose-kon-gan-dew-leis-kon-cos-tee-yi-tas-day-sur-dou—did I get it right, my dear?"

"Ummm, yeah… Absolutely!"

"As we learned from today's guest, this is a dish you will find in many Puerto Rican households during the holidays, particularly Nochebuena. That's Christmas Eve en español, my friends. But like all good rice recipes, the dish works all year round."

"So, how's this for an idea? Try a side of arroz con whatevers for your next Labor Day cook-out and amaze your family. Don't forget to pair it with the delicious Xavier's Gift of Chocolate mousse, the recipe courtesy of Felipe Sánchez, one of Naples' best dessert chefs. And if you don't tell that the secret is avocadoes, I won't tell either! Again, I'd like to thank my guest, Cici Citroën—"

"Cintron."

"*Désolée*, darling. Again, my thanks to Cici, a recent New Jersey transplant to our beautiful city, for sharing her family recipe. And thank you, all of you, my lovies, for viewing and subscribing and recommending Maureen's Kitchen to all the cooks in your life."

"Don't forget to visit us at least once a week. At Maureen's Kitchen, we pride ourselves in being a happy, relaxed space where we learn about cooking delicious foods with a Florida twist. And the occasional household tip.

"Today's, in fact, was inspired by this amazing coconut lime candle I lit in honor of today's culinary theme. Remember to click on the link below, where you can buy this gorgeous Caribbean-inspired beauty. One lucky lovey will be gifted one this week. Doesn't it smell yummy, Cici?"

"I'm not a huge fan of—"

"Oh, you! So here we are. Our delicious candle looks like it's done, but there's still a good amount of wax at the bottom. Do we have to throw it out? No, we don't! Candlewicks are cheap and available by the hundreds at many craft stores. See the puddle at the bottom? Just drop in a new wick and trim for length. Be very careful, though. It might be hot. And there we are, back in candle business!

"Because, as we always say around Maureen's Kitchen, who's got money to burn?"

***

I was one with the Universe, no question about it. At every moment this morning, it was as if a new force flowed through me, directing every one of my words, my gestures, my movements. I do realize it will be a lot of work, posting often, and keeping it fresh, as Ayesha reminded me as they left, but I am more than ready for that challenge.

Namaste, Universe, for opening this path for me. I bow in gratitude to the life force who keeps me and mine safe. The life force who sent new, interesting people my way in the middle of tragedy. Yes, I am not forgetting how Betty and Cici, too, came into my life. But for today, no sadness, only positivity.

"Right, Bertie? Don't you look particularly fetching today? I bet you'd look adorable in one of those tiara and tutu combos. Why should bulldogs corner the market on cuteness? I could even post it on our page! Another way to brand us, as Shaggy insists.

"Our retro cottage and you, our alpha Canis Majoris, the brightest star of the night sky. Oh, Bertie, for those nights of spotting stars with Gian." I put down my phone with another sigh. I then delete the "Shop for outfits for Bertie" note from my Reminders.

"Ollie's bound to murder me in some hideous, impossible-to-detect way if she even caught a whiff that I put you in a tiara. I suppose we'll have to make do with you helping me pick out my outfit. I'm so happy. I want to look extra spiffy to Betty's."

Just then, Bertie leaves my side and goes lie down in

the shadiest corner of the bedroom. As usual, for July, it is inhumanly humid in here. Chicago-in-February-don't-go out levels of awful. Even with the help of all the trees around the property, the ancient air conditioner barely cools the air in here.

Ollie's room must truly be hell. But then, she wanted to face the street. No doubt she thinks she's keeping the neighborhood safe. Her and her *leetle* grey cells. It must've been great fun, those days of the flag of a martini glass we found in her closet, hanging from the pole outside her window: "Come in and have a drink." At least, back in the fifties, the cottage had air by then. How did Mr. O'Bryan and his associates endure business meetings down here in the summer before it was installed? I can't even begin to imagine.

"Still, how cool was that, uh, darling?" I threw over my shoulder at Bertie. "Personal maids to lay the wives evening outfits, then dinner at the Naples Hotel, down the way. Low-waisted frocks, a tiara across your forehead, and rows of pearls. Can you just imagine? Too, too, divine. Then again, you had to come back to sleep here, with only the open, screened windows for ventilation, so there's that.

"There! There's that sound again, Bertie! Did you hear it?"

First the Granny, now the AC wheezing away. I don't want to think what will happen if…. Nope, nopetty nope, no, ma'am. Positive thoughts, only for today. Plus, the sun is beginning to go down. And Betty's house is bound to be nice and cold.

Here goes nothing. My Italian straw bag, my Canfora sandals, and my sleeveless Pucci midi. Apricot and white circles on an icy blue background so refreshing. "Oh, Bertie, I wish you'd known Capri back then."

And if the knit stretches out a bit much at the hips, and the arms are not what they once were, so be it. Again, if only for today, positive thoughts all around me.

***

Betty's welcome is as warm as ever. She truly is an old soul. I know we've known each other for several lifetimes. When she leaves towards what I assume is the kitchen area with another contribution to the dinner menu—that coconut flan she liked so much—I take the opportunity to examine my surroundings carefully.

To be honest, I did check it out the first time I was here, but I could be forgiven for missing out on some of the details, given the hideous injuries I had just sustained. Injuries the extent of which I bravely kept to myself, I note in passing in case I need to remind Ollie in the days to come.

"Oooo, stark white walls and glossy black trim. I love it!" I say as Betty ushers us towards the back of the living room, with its floor to ceiling windows. "Is that Ball and Farrow paint?"

"Yeah. But don't ask me for the color because I have no clue. All I know is it's like living inside a tasty coconut."

When I step through the door to the back, I am momentarily deprived of speech. An infinity pool fronts the sea. At the edge of the wide blue expanse are wicker chairs that look like a sideways S, arrayed on a checkboard pattern on square spaces of gold and navy glass tile, under which water flows serenely. The area around the pool, alone, is huge, easily, space for two-hundred guests. To our right is another sitting section, this one covered, and surrounded by tall terracotta vases with plantings, set with teak and cane furniture. All of it, a symphony of stark, clean lines, set against the impossible blue hues of the Gulf and the sky. The epitome of mid-century modern design, updated for our day. It fits the rest of the house décor faultlessly.

Still busy taking mental notes—wait till I call Alison in Palm Springs. She's the Modernist fan— I realize I missed the approach of a man from the back of the covered area.

"Let me guess. You must be Maureen," he says as he comes to a stop before us. "I'm Manny."

BETTY

"Charles Manuel on the birth certificate. Manny to everybody these days." I hear him repeat the introduction as he turns towards Ollie. My two friends remain silent for a few seconds. I suppose with all the hullabaloo in the news over the sale of Manny's last year, it makes for a big surprise when people finally meet him. Not anybody's image of a corporate tycoon by any stretch of the imagination.

Oh, I adore the man. But I know well what they see. An average guy in his early sixties, medium tall, with a thatch of silver hair that matches a pair of grey eyes, made more translucent by a deep tan. And then there's his hands, square and blunt. One look, and you know you can place your life in his care.

Finally, face to face with the two women he's heard so much about lately, my husband then does that *thing* he's not even aware he does when meeting interesting people. He tilts his head slightly to the left, and leans a bit forward, the better to stare into their eyes, and the next moment, even Ollie stands taller.

It's the unconscious move of somebody who truly engages with others. Not just everybody, of course. But when you have Manny's attention, it's like basking in a warm pool of light on a chilly day.

Handshakes and introductions over, we move towards the covered seating area. The sunset is still a couple of hours away, and the humidity is at its all-time high. The only consolation to be had is that the afternoon showers unleashed competing scents from the nearby basil and oregano planters, aromas that still hang heavily in the air.

I escort Ollie, who seems all too willing to escape the heat generated by that uncomfortable sling. Poor Ollie, what a time to be strapped into that contraption, July in Florida.

A batch of mojitos, ready to be poured into frosty glasses, awaits us. I join the sisters as Manny begins to fuss with the contents of the refrigerator. Boy, does the man love to show off his cooking skills. Not a competitor to Maureen's gourmet kitchen by any means, but still. My husband likes to make sure our guests don't think it's all brats around the Manuel household.

***

"Now, *this* is sushi-grade tuna!" declares Maureen, just a few minutes into the appetizers. "Excellent tuna tartare, Manny."

"Amazing, amazing," pipes up Ollie. At least, that's what I think she says. She's still busy chewing. Glad to see her momentary left-handedness doesn't hinder her efforts.

"I know when I must step up my game, ladies. I heard about the menu at your place the other night. What was it, Betts?"

"Those cucumber boats with peanuts and chili powder? The homemade tortilla chips? Two different kinds of flan? I can't remember when I've made a bigger pig of myself."

"See what I mean, ladies? I wasn't about to sleep in the porch with the puppies today. Isn't that one of Freddy's?" he adds in my direction. Manny then throws back his head with a deep laugh. It does my heart good to see him so at ease with my new friends, enjoying their company as much as I do.

"One of Freddy's favorite sayings," I clarify for our mystified guests. "If you can't keep up with the big dogs, you gotta sleep in the porch with the puppies."

"Well, from what I saw out there, dogs around here enjoy lovely accommodations," Ollie chimes in, finally done chewing. She points with her thumb to the front of the house, where Manny's RV is parked on the driveway.

"Oh, you mean the *Bow Wow? Brats Wow!?* That's home away from home." Two faces look up at him with expectant smiles, awaiting an explanation. "Betty didn't tell you?"

"We've been otherwise engaged this week," I chuckle, shaking my head. "And it wasn't canasta at the country club, either."

"Don't remind me, please. I'm having a blast," Manny says, throwing his hands up in the hair. "The RV is my command center-slash-home for my days on the road," he adds, turning to Ollie and Maureen then. "I race cars. Or rather, me and my team do. Talk about your puppies. Manuel Racing is the newest kid on a very crowded block.

"Hey, I have an idea!" he yelps, sitting up straight. "Maybe you'd like to go with us to the next Daytona? You ladies can keep Betts company. In a hotel suite, of course. We'd love to have you as our guests."

The suggestion hangs in the air for a few seconds while Maureen and Ollie diplomatically busy themselves with the appetizers remaining on their plates. The thought of fashionable Maureen and literary Ollie at the NASCAR races strikes me as funny, but then stranger things have happened in my life lately. And who knows, maybe they're huge fans of car racing. In any case, who knows where we will be next February?

I stifle a smile, all the same, as I go about collecting dishes. Manny meanwhile turns to the barbecue, all the covered dishes close at hand. To be fair, to call that thing a *barbecue* is another throwback to the summer days of my childhood, some still chilly when a couple of hot dogs and chicken legs simmered on a tiny grill.

Manny's barbecue looks like it can communicate with NASA. I'm expecting any day now, it will take off into orbit.

I realize then I'm a little giddy from the mojitos, and I stifle a hiccup. That doesn't stop me from bringing out the wine that's been awaiting, already decanted.

The menu was a success, but then, few people of my acquaintance are unhappy with lobster or steak. Even my vegan daughter has been known to make an exception for the former. Among the offerings are some lobster kebabs, too, to make eating easier for Ollie, who still looked mutinous when Maureen insisted on taking them off the skewers for her. Ollie still had the grace to bite back any retorts, however, as Maureen placed the plate in front of her with a very maternal, "There you go, sweetheart."

These two kill me. They really do. One minute, they remind me of the cats in a childhood cartoon. A ball of hissing and spitting fur flying around. Next, you realize they are each other's best friends. Life partners as only sisters can be. Me? I'm happy to be a small moon orbiting in the path of their suns.

Oh, my, I am giddier than I thought I was. A realization not helped when Manny brings out two bottles of rosé champagne with the pound cake *and* the flan to welcoming smiles all around, particularly Maureen's. Served with a bowl of strawberries and good old-fashioned vanilla and chocolate ice cream, the desserts are the perfect ending to a summer meal.

"How did you know pound cake is my favorite?" Manny winks over his second slice.

"I didn't know," Maureen answers, an answering glint in her eye.

"Now you do," he ripostes with a wink. "And June 13th is my birthday. I'll have Betty remind you."

"No need, done and done!" Maureen laughs back, putting her phone away. "I'd remind you of mine, but I've stopped having any more of those,"

Over espresso, my husband grows sentimental, as he often does in good company. "So happy to welcome you to our home, which I hope you'll consider yours from now on," he says, lifting the small cup in their direction. "So happy to see you all safe."

"Delighted to be here, too," Ollie answers with a short bow. Given Ollie's character, however, I'm not really surprised when she adds next. "Delighted we finally got to meet you, Manny. I only wish it had been under happier circumstances. If only we could've prevented that man's criminal rampage."

"How could we?" This is from me, but Maureen nods energetically at my words. "Even the police didn't link the two. Had it not been for us, they'd still be looking at the robbery and the murder as two separate incidents."

"Still, there were omissions on our part, dear Betty. Terrible omissions." Ollie holds up the fingers of her left hand, the better to underscore her answer. "First, Mo and I failed to tell the police about DeSant being on the pier early on."

"Second, and this one's totally on me, I stopped by the parking lot when I found out about the hit-and-run. I could tell that whatever car hit young Xavier had probably ended up damaged. But I was thrown for a loop when I heard the police had been to see you."

"Oh, my, yes," breathes in Maureen, sobered up momentarily by the sad account.

Now it's my turn. I shake my head. "And I hear rumors about his business trouble, but I was too tipsy to pass them on..."

The three of us pause for a second, the happy mood in danger of being destroyed, only to hear Manny chime in. "At the risk of sounding like a mansplainer, your biggest mistake was in trying to take on that SOB on your own. What were you thinking, ladies?"

Regrets silences us momentarily, only to have Maureen

straighten up a second later in her seat. Gone is the momentary dismay. She reminds me now of those toys that get hit and bounce happily back.

"We'll do better next time!"

"There's not going to be a next time. What is wrong with you, Mo? The essence of detecting is remembering and putting pieces together. At our age? Please!"

I can tell Manny is about to start laughing at the expressions on both their faces, so I step in. My husband can wait a little longer to get the full "cartoon cats" effect from the sisters.

"Ladies, what are the odds anything like this will happen to us again? Let's concentrate on the here and now. Maureen, you said you had some inquiries?"

"Yes, I did! Just this morning, before the taping. A couple of phone calls from rental companies."

"Two of the best in town," pipes Ollie with a proud grin.

"They'd like to talk to me. Hire-a-vacation-chef, I called it in my description. I'd left messages around town, but nothing. Not a response."

"And then we're in the local news," Ollie picks up while Maureen pauses for a draught of champagne, "and the next thing you know, they come a-calling. I suppose the adage is true. There's no such thing as bad publicity."

"Just a couple of fingers. What the heck. Go ahead, don't let it go to waste," Maureen adds as Manny tips the bottle over the flute. "I'm seeing them day after tomorrow, but I still don't have a name for the company!

"The name of the blog, I've become a vlogger, in case you haven't heard," she offers in Manny's direction, "is solved. Maureen's Kitchen, easy to remember. But I want something memorable for the chief gig, Magical Mystery Tour memorable."

"How about the Mystery Machine? We already have a Shaggy. Let's collect the set," Ollie retorts with a straight face.

"What do people call you? Do you have a nickname?" This from Manny, a second later, his game face firmly on.

"No nicknames, except Mo. And I'm not using that!"

"How about your kids? What do they call you?"

"My kids call me Mama Bear—"

"Hear, hear," says Ollie, with a slight roll of her eyes.

"And then there's Mimi. My grandkids call me Mimi."

"Well, how about Mimi's Movable Feast?"

"I like that. It's got a certain flair, *n'est-ce pas*?" There are Rs thrown with abandon with the *flair* to go with the French at the end. In response, we hear a faint but unmistakable groan from Ollie.

"Very well, Ms. Smarty Pants," Maureen counters, turning to her sister, a sunny grin on her face. "Why don't you tell them what you're up to?"

And then, to my utter surprise, Ollie becomes a different person than the woman I've come to know this past week. Suddenly abashed, she seems all too ready to step hide from the limelight for once.

"I've decided to pursue a recent idea of mine," she finally says with a sigh, batting Maureen's prodding elbow away. "I'm writing a mystery. There, happy now?" This last is directed at Maureen, who pats her hand.

"Our very own Jessica Fletcher!"

"Oh, Naples already has one of those, the redoubtable Stratemeyer," Ollie retorts in response to my words. "And unwilling to cede the scepter. Although, I guess I shouldn't grouse. Harriet's offered to help with agents. She's been very helpful."

"Well, anyway, congratulations, Ollie," I offer, remembering the striking woman at the memorial service. "Both of you, in fact. Look at you both, pursuing your dreams.

You're an inspiration, the way you're reinventing yourselves."

"Hold on, hold on, and yes, congrats all around, my friends. Never easy to start something from scratch. I should know," this from Manny, who clinks each sister's glass with a bow. "But if we're going to talk reinvention, how about you, Betts?"

Ever loyal, my husband goes on, when I remain silent. "In between all this craziness, Betty's gone forward with a project of hers. Long in planning, true, but here we finally have it turned into a reality. The Counting on You Foundation. How does it go, Betts?"

"Offering financial literacy classes and math tutoring for people of all ages, particularly children, K-12 and their parents," I quote from memory. "There will also be college aid, as long as one custodial adult signs up for a couple of financial literacy sessions."

I loved hearing Manny's words, but I wish he had waited a little longer for the announcement. Today, I don't want anything to take away the spotlight from my friends' ventures. But I continue, and as I speak, I realize the truth of my words.

"You two lit the spark. Manny's right. We had both long wanted to do something, given our immense luck. But it was meeting you two, that got me off my duff and pushed me to the finish line. I'd still be feeling sorry for the loss of my old role in the company if I hadn't met you that day at the pier."

"So, thank you. Thanks for all you've brought into my life. Including a bit of unexpected mayhem, yes."

"Good trouble, yes. Of the best kind, getting that murderous cretin off the streets," Ollie says, tapping the table.

"And before you say a word about the reward," I warn them, having already heard from Maureen on the phone what the detective had to say on that topic, "let me tell you, I'm not taking a cent. But I will accept a donation," I pause to the count of three, "to establish a scholarship in Xavier's name. Consider that my share of the money."

"Fair is fair," agrees Ollie, back to her formal self. "We did say, all in. Three ways, or no way."

"That will be the first donation to the foundation, in fact," I nod in agreement.

"Dear me, this is all so exciting," Maureen chimes in, holding her flute up as she looks around. "Betty, dearest, does that mean you'll be planning...ahem...galas? Fund-raising galas? This is the perfect space for them."

"Standard procedure, Mo. All foundations have them. Why? You're not thinking of pursuing romantic liaisons by the pool, are you?"

"Why, Ollie Howard. What did I say about you making odious comments about my love life last time we were here?"

And they're off. Except this time, the bickering is interrupted by the appearance of Manny, another bottle of champagne in hand. Ignoring the sputtering sounds coming from both the sisters, like a couple of tea kettles on boil, he refills the flutes all around.

He then stands before his seat at the table and stares deeply into my eyes.

"To my beautiful wife. To the best of sisters ever," he intones next, with a gallant bow in my friends' direction. "To smart women everywhere."

I swear, he waited just for this moment. No sooner has Manny finished bowing, that the sky over the Naples Pier bursts into a jewelry box of greens, reds, oranges, and silver. We ohh and ahh for a few seconds, faces turned upwards like happy children. Who doesn't feel like a kid again watching Fourth of July fireworks?

"To friends," I continue after a few seconds, raising my voice over the explosions. Ollie and Maureen lift their flutes, and then, a couple of wide smiles form on both their faces.

"To friends, the jewels of life. Without them, life is poor. No matter how rich you are."

"I'll drink to that," the sister responded at the same time. And so, we did.

OLLIE

It was my turn to put Mo to bed. Oh, it wasn't the dinner at the Manuel's. She kept her head, even though that rosé champagne is very much her particular downfall. I believe it was that haze of unreality that comes from having a long-held dream finally come true. Not only is Mo's blog up and running, but her vacation chef also-for-hire scheme has gained some traction among local rental agencies. I overheard her on the phone as I came down earlier this morning but was unable to hear all the details until we go to Betty's this evening.

The business of shadowing Ayesha and Shaggy and taking notes single-handed kept me on my toes this morning. I was scheduled to handle the blog on my own today, but now that I am out of commission, the kids will keep it going for a while.

On that topic, according to our young friends, Mo would be enormously lucky if she achieved that coveted modern title of "social media influencer." Go figure. There's even talk of creating some sort of dance on the TikTok, all the better to catch the public's fickle attention. I will run a discreet veil over what I think of *that* idea. Although, if I know my sister, she'll probably be practicing her moves first thing tomorrow.

I take one last look at Mo, lost in that sea of embroidered pillows she insists on keeping on her bed. She went down like a toddler. One minute, buzzing around like teeny insane elf; the next second, down on the floor, juicy cup still in their drooling mouth.

Then again, Mo and toddlers share the same propensity for abandoning their beds, full of vim and vigor, before calmer heads are ready for the day.

In the dimness of my sister's room, as I'm about to turn the last light off, I can hear Bert's claws clicking on the wooden floor beside me. I also notice a distinct doggie aroma in the way-too-warm air. Please, please, please, by all the gods, don't let it be the AC. With a sinking feeling it is very much the AC, I then seek the refuge of my nighttime reading.

It is too hot for a cup of chai but never too warm for sweets, despite the feast to which we were treated by Manny Manuel. Interesting man. Amazingly, despite his past business success, he bears no trace of being a Blanche, a virtue I totally attribute to his wife's good sense.

Moving quietly, my faithful companion by my side, I place the leftover oatmeal cookies I found on a platter with some awkwardness. Damn sling. I suppose I shouldn't begrudge Cici the dozen treats Mo insisted on wrapping for her after the taping. Not much, I don't.

Bert, enjoying a couple of treats I threw his way, seems to agree with me. "Good dog!" Crumbs trail both our steps as I finally gain my reading chair — that trusty, old friend — and reach for my laptop. Before I flip the screen open, however, I grab one of the rulers I liberated from the dining table that has become my sister's desk.

"There, much better," I whisper to Bert, ever attentive by my side, as I apply it to the underside of my arm. "Dinosaurs that change colors when you move the ruler, I ask you…"

Having dealt with the problem, I then secrete the item again between the pillow and the armchair arm. Yes, faulty AC or not, life promises to be quite interesting soon. Not only is Mo's business about to take off, but my own plans have also moved one step further.

Harriet has agreed to read my manuscript as soon as

she is done with a series of online interviews for her latest thriller. Not up to Poirot's standards, in my opinion, but a good series nonetheless, her Haoyu "Hank" Lee, the scourge of the San Francisco tongs, often partnered by the redoubtable Sam Spade.

"Welcome to the fight, Olympia," she boomed with a hearty laugh. Drat the woman. I suppose convincing her to call me by my chosen name will have to wait for the right moment. She also mentioned she would introduce me to a local writers' workshop. "A battery of barracudas, but the feedback is good," she promised. "If you have a couple of hours to spare and a thick skin. Well worth it."

Oh, mine is plenty thick, thank you very much. As for time, I have ample time at my disposal these days.

I'll be taking some time off, as per the doctor's suggestion. Unwilling to wait until I return, of course, my colleagues have visited in droves, wanting the gory details of the crime, of which I have been more than happy to supply. Rosa also reports that my injuries, incurred while apprehending a murderer, are the topic de jour at the staff room in the library. As well as our patrons.

Not that I'm one to brag, unlike my sister and her "life-saving phone" or some such. My supervisor, too, has been enormously understanding. "Take all the time you need, dear. That search can wait."

Given my new resolution to be more accommodating of other people's foibles — case in point, Harriet Stratemeyer's — I decided not to voice the reply that cropped immediately to mind. "Searches cannot wait. What are we, Congress?"

In the meantime, no time like the present, do or die, yadda, yadda, yadda. Which is to say, all the cookies disposed of. I open a new document and stare at the blank page for a few seconds. I lick my lips, where the sweet taste of cinnamon and raisins lingers, and flex the fingers of my left hand. "Here we go, Bert! The game is afoot!"

It had been a disappointing afternoon at whist when Lady Maura received the latest bill from the apothecary. Newly impoverished, the London beauty feared she must leave her home on Belgrade Square. Turning to her sister Odette?, Odile?, Ophir? Ophelia! the Lady Ophelia, newly graduated from Lady Margaret Hall at Oxford...

INTERLUDE #5

With the help of a cottier yclept Maurice and his brother, who lays claim to the unlikely title of the Chevalier, the perimeter of the keep has finally been secured. I have recruited a host of nearby denizens and trained them in the proper use of arms. While rustics, methinks they will make for a stalwart thithing.

As usual, I expect no gratitude from the harridans amongst whom I find myself reduced these days. The Uncommonly Tall One continues to peck away at the large metal casket. The Midge is nowhere to be found. She has probably retired to her bower and the bed that I, in my magnificence, allow her to share.

Hark! The phrase "Tortoni, tomorrow. Got it! Wait until...garble garble...hears about this," draws my attention. That varlet, again!

The Uncommonly Tall One continues to yammer away at a small coffer in her hand for the length of a Paternoster. Such are the heathenish customs of these parts.

On that point, betwixt the levying of the host and the sorties against that poltroon of a town crier, I have made no progress ascertaining whose cunning magik is behind my present pitiful circumstances.

Could the dastardly hand that cast mine ensorcellment be that of a female? It does not bear thinking, but I did detect the most unusual smell in the keep, thrice thus far. A womanly aroma in combination with the chivalrous scent of a constable's weaponry.

But how could it be thus? What world of insanity would that be, a shire reduced to the enforcement of its laws by a female sheriff?

Heavens forfend, should that unlikely event prove to be the case, it is a clutch of powerful daughters of Belial I now face. Well, mine, yeomen. A knight of my rank must save his efforts for planning battles and winning adepts in court.

Comforted by that thought, for the nonce, I cast a look around me and settle for the evening. Avaunt, shadows! No time for pusillanimity, this. My cause is just, and I will prevail. By my troth, I will. Or my name isn't Bertram, Seigneur de la Bouillon Chaude. Valenter volenter!

THE END

A former academic at a university in Chicago, Olivia Viyella has been a reader of mysteries and a teller of tales, some of them true, ever since childhood. She is the mother of two strong, take-no-prisoners daughters, a lucky wife, a sister, and the sort of friend you'd call when rope and shovels are necessary.

In her retirement, she divides her time between Naples, Florida, and a Chicago suburb.